To Jeffrey,

Very best wishes,

Dirk Rudgen

October 2o5

Bad day for a fat boy

Dirk Robertson

Published by
The X Press
PO Box 25694
London, N17 6FP
Tel: 020 8801 2100
Fax: 020 8885 1322
E-mail: vibes@xpress.co.uk
Web site: www.xpress.co.uk

© Dirk Robertson 2003

The right of Dirk Robertson to be identified as the author of this work has been asserted in accordance with the Copyright, Designs and Patents Act 1988.

The characters and situations in this book are entirely imaginary and bear no relation to any real person or actual happenings.

This book is sold subject to the condition that it shall not, by way of trade or otherwise, be lent, re-sold, hired out or otherwise circulated without the publisher's prior consent in any form of binding or cover other than that in which it is published and without a similar condition including this condition being imposed on the subsequent purchaser.

No part of this publication may be reproduced or transmitted in any form or by any means, electronic or mechanical, including photocopying, recording or any information storage or retrieval system, without either the prior permission in writing from the publisher or a license, permitting restricted copying.

Printed by Cox & Wyman, Reading, UK

Distributed in UK by Turnaround Distribution
Unit 3, Olympia Trading Estate, Coburg Road, London N22 6TZ
Tel: 020 8829 3000
Fax: 020 8881 5088

ISBN 1-902934-19-9

Bad day for a fat boy

ABOUT THE AUTHOR

Dirk Robertson was born and lives in Edinburgh, Scotland. His first novel Highland T'ing, published by The X Press was nominated for the Silver Dagger crime writing awards and received critical acclaim. Currently working as a full time writer, Dirk is among many things, a black belt Karate instructor and a qualified social worker. *Bad Day for a Fat Boy* is is second novel and he is currently working on his third book.

Bad day for a fat boy

There's a lot of people I'd like to express my appreciation to. I'll keep it to Stella, and The X-Press.
(Sounds like the title of a book.)

THE SHIP HEAVED LIKE A FAT OLD DRUNK gorged on rice wine. It shouldn't have been out in this weather. The South China Sea gives no favours and tonight Typhoon "Charlie" was in an evil mood. Mi-Lei checked the clip of his harness which was lashed to the outer rail. Experience had taught him that in a storm everything had to be attached to something metal, welded and with a bolt the size of a horse's dick through it. He was on the second watch and though he had been outside for only a few moments he was already soaked. The storm was so loud, it felt as though his eardrums were going to burst. A tough hardy sailor, he felt something tonight which hadn't visited him for many moons. Genuine, heart stopping, mouth rasping fear. His mouth was dry and his throat felt like it had been massaged with a cheese grater. If someone had offered him a cold wet beer, he would fallen on it like a newborn to its mother's breast. He couldn't swallow and his heart was pumping so much he half expected it to burst out of his chest onto the deck in front of him. He feared not only the weather, but for his very soul. He shouldn't have been out on this job tonight, but he needed the money and the boys were not the kind of people who appreciated the word "no."

A massive crack of lightning illuminated the ship as it fell fifty feet from the bow of a wave onto the sea below. It hit with a sickening thud and bounced like a ball on concrete. Mi-Lei thought of his wife and little boy and could feel the salt of his tears mix with the saltwater of the Fuzian Straits. He had travelled this stretch of water, which runs between Taiwan and mainland China, many times but tonight he made himself a promise. He vowed that this would be his last trip ever on "The Happy Dancer." It's important to be careful what you dream for in this life, as sometimes it comes true. That's not always a good thing. He didn't know it, but tonight Mi-Lei was going to find that out.

A huge wave hit the grain ship and it shifted sideways to be smashed by an even bigger wall of water. Mi-Lei's harness suddenly snapped like a rotten twig and he was swept down the steps, spinning onto the lower decks. One of the hold covers had fractured and he could hear a wailing sound, clearly audible even above the whining and screaming of the evil winds. His head hung over the lip of the hold. He couldn't move even if he'd wanted to due to the massive force which was now gripping the ship. His spine was broken in three places and he was pinned to the spot, like an insect on a collector's tray.

Another crack of lightning lit up the hold and revealed the source of the strange noise—three hundred shining, sweat streaked faces, their necks straining toward the moon. Men, women, and children paralysed with fear and stricken with pain, were still hopeful that a new life awaited them on the other side of this wild storm. That was the last thing Mi-Lei would ever see. The ship broke apart like a matchstick model as, with a roar like a gorgon, a seventy foot wave slapped it below the sealine. People, metal, and broken dreams spiralled to the bottom of the sea, where some kind of hell and some kind of heaven waited for them all. Another crack of lightning lit up the sky. The swollen sea was now empty. There was no sign that the ship, or its cargo of lost souls, had ever existed at all.

2

"I'm nobody!" Milly said quietly and precisely through mouthfuls of breakfast. A little streak of marmite by the side of her mouth meant it was unnecessary to ask what had been spread on the toast. She looked like she was smiling despite the gravity of her announcement. Her round blue eyes twinkled out of a clear smooth face sitting under a head of tight blond curls. Murray Kennedy was taken aback and stroked the two day old stubble on his chin. If he looked fatherly and concerned, it's because he was both. It seemed to have little effect on his three year old. Without blinking she just held his gaze. There had been a Friday night TV show recently with children competing to see who would blink first in a staring competition. If Murray remembered correctly the child could win lots of prizes (like cars and boats) for their parents. Milly would have swept the board if she'd been entered. The show had been axed for being in really bad taste, with little kids breaking down and crying when they failed to win for their mums and dads. Just as well the show had been cancelled, there wasn't enough room for a boat in the driveway of Kennedy's small home in what used to be known as the cheaper part of Islington. Now, the whole borough stank of expensive real estate. A property agent would probably have called it well-appointed. After all, it was near enough so that on a clear day you could see all the way to Hackney, but far enough away so that the smell of cordite from another drug dealer's angry weapon, wouldn't reach you. Still, it could always be passed off as just a bad smell from the timber yard next door. Murray had written a few letters to the council to enquire why a noisy yard with all its blowing sawdust and crap was able to open up in a residential area. All he'd got back so far was a letter written on cheap paper, curled at the edges, and looking as though someone had carried it around in their bottom for days, before posting it. It said that they were looking into it, which translated meant that a stuff was not given and they weren't.

Beverley came into the kitchen and proceeded to wipe her hands on the slightly stained kitchen towel. She'd picked it up from the floor where it landed after losing the struggle to stay on the overloaded peg nailed clumsily to the back of the pine door. At thirty, she was nine years younger than Kennedy and a whole lot more shapely. Of mixed parentage, she was well-built with some very becoming freckles on her face. Bright laughing hazel eyes meant that there was seldom a time when she did not receive attention from members of the opposite sex, the same sex, and some in-between.

She'd started off as the next-door neighbour, then became a real friend after Kennedy lost his wife, Debbie. A short-sighted and nervous old driver on a cold rainy night on Upper street made an illegal u-turn just when Murray and Debbie were crossing on the green man. The front end had hit Debbie. She'd died instantly said the doctor, as if it was meant to be some kind of consolation. It wasn't. The back end had hit Kennedy a glancing blow with just enough force to ruin his left arm and to end his career as a professional musician. For a full six months after Debbie's death, he lay under a stinking duvet with a bottle of Jack Daniels. Then Beverley had come into his front room, his bedroom, and finally his life. She had firmly but gently reminded him that there wasn't just himself to think of, there was Milly too. Her mixture of South London humour and Jamaican firmness had been a real blessing. It had also made sure that they had ended up becoming more than just next-door neighbours. Hers was an attraction which many men found they were unable or unwilling to resist. Murray Kennedy was no exception. But without a doubt, the death of his wife and all that went with it was the worst thing that could possibly have happened to him, or so he thought.

Beverley finished drying her hands and kissed her teeth. Kissed rather than sucked. There is a difference. She did that whether she was pleased or just making a point. Whatever, it always got Kennedy's attention.

"What's up? You look a bit off." She examined her finger nails as she spoke.

Kennedy sighed and nodded at Milly, who was sitting quite still. Beverley went over to her and wiped some of the marmite off her face. Her brightly coloured fingernails glittered in the stream of sunlight coming through the frost covered window.

"You alright, Sweetheart?"

"I'm nobody." Milly fixed Beverley with the same firm stare. Beverley took a piece of toast off Milly's plate.

"No, you're somebody, darling." She shot a concerned look at Kennedy who raised his eyebrows. He had two distinct ones. He was now at the age where he had to shave the middle one. Unfortunately, like a lot of older men, if he didn't tackle it with a razor he looked like a werewolf with one giant eyebrow stretching from eye to eye. Designer stubble does not work anywhere near the eyes.

"No, I'm not. I'm nobody." Milly didn't look upset but the steely determined tone in her voice was unmistakable.

Beverley smiled and turned to Murray. "What does Mister Max think?" She said, as she went to the toaster and popped a couple of slices of fresh grain bread in and set the dial to medium.

Kennedy grimaced and spoke through gritted teeth. "I

haven't a clue what Mister Max thinks."

Beverley spoke slowly and precisely as though she was speaking to someone who was even younger than Milly. "Well, why don't you ask him?"

Kennedy licked his lips and walked over to the table. He sat down next to the stuffed toy sitting on Milly's left. It had a smiling happy face, a full head of something which had possibly once passed for hair and a stripy little suit which made it look like an old-fashioned convict. Mister Max also had an eye missing as a result of Milly thinking Beverley's dog might like to kiss him.

Rex was a Rotweiler. Some years ago, he was given to Beverley as a puppy; a gift from her brother Ray. Ray was a rude boy, a South London geezer with rules and principles not shared by London's finest. But he was, what he was. One early morning some perv had tried to attack Beverley while she was out jogging near Manor Park. Beverley had been lucky, she was stronger than she looked and when she'd lashed out the nonce had gotten a fright. After that she'd legged it and left him far behind. Nature had been on her side. It's not that easy to run with a stonking great erection sticking out of your strides.

Ray was upset, and so he'd bought Rex from a bloke in Bermondsey to protect his sister on her outings. It turned out to be a wise investment. Rex had been a jolly little puppy, with a lick for everyone. Now he was many stone of snot and muscle with an ingrained appetite for uncooked human flesh and a hatred of men deep enough to get him instant membership in the local feminist group.

That wasn't quite the end of it though. Ray was well-known round quite a few different parts of London and he couldn't let it be known that he hadn't given out some street justice. As far as he was concerned all the pervs lived in North London, so the guy who had preyed on his kid sister wouldn't be that hard to find. Beverley's experience had reinforced his view that all the weirdos resided North of the Thames. North, South, whatever, honour had been at stake. You don't try to rip off Ray Winter's sister's panties and think you are going to get away with it. Seems the bloke was quite well known for hanging around the park and nicking women's' undies off washing lines. It didn't take much detective work to find him. Once they did, Ray's bredrin, Lex and Ice got to work on him. Nothing too heavy, just a bit of a sorting out one cold and windy night up an alley, not far from the scene of his crime. A broken jaw, a couple of kicks in the bollocks, a smack in the head, all enough to show him the error of his pervy ways. Bit like sexual therapy so to speak. Beverley had been pretty upset once she'd got wind of what had transpired, but calmed down when she realised that the damage wasn't permanent, just enough to shrink the hard-on and to convince him of the desirability of a change of address.

With regard to Kennedy, Ray wasn't too keen on the black-white thing. The white guys always seemed to get the best part of the deal, he didn't see them trying to check out the ugly sisters. Basically, he felt that Beverley could do better, that Murray was a bit needy with the loss of his wife and all that. It wasn't that Ray was unsympathetic to his loss just that he was not willing to compromise when it came to his sister's happiness and well-being.

"What do you think, Mister Max?" Kennedy tried hard not to patronise the puppet. It wasn't easy. Mister Max stared back at him with the good eye.

"Daddy?" Milly spoke slowly and surely, a bit like Beverley had done. Suddenly Kennedy felt as though he was the youngest person in the room, apart from Mister Max, who seemed to have aged a bit. Must have been the trauma of the unwanted attention from Rex.

"Yes?" He smiled at his daughter.

"Why are you asking Mister Max what he thinks?"

"Because I care, darling." Kennedy felt pleased with

himself. Somehow that answer seemed right.

"But, Daddy..." Milly sighed, "Mister Max can't speak. You know that."

The smile on Kennedy's face faded, just like his old denim shirt with the top button missing. He nodded slowly and stood up. Beverley raised her eyebrows. She gestured to the front room. Kennedy followed her out of the kitchen into the tastefully decorated living room. It had souvenirs from the many journeys he'd made all around the world.

"You've got a problem, here." Beverley said with some understatement.

"What do you think I should do? She doesn't look upset." Kennedy shook his head and pursed his lips, his eyebrows knitted together; just as well he'd shaved.

"You're not spending enough time with her." She adopted that prim school teacher pose which Kennedy hated. Arms folded, brow furrowed and one leg cocked against the other. "In fact..." she continued before he could reply, "you're not spending enough time with either of us."

It was a statement not a question. He'd known this was going to come, he just hadn't expected it today. Beverley had been a tower of strength for him and Milly, ever since that awful night he'd lost Debbie. She was as fine a woman any man could hope for, but there was something inside Kennedy which stopped him from letting himself go. His emotions had been ripped apart as though they had been dragged through razor-wire. His spirit had not properly recovered; he wasn't sure if it ever would. This was a very real and awkward barrier to developing a proper relationship with Beverley even though she certainly deserved one.

The trouble was it was so hard to talk about. Every time he tried, the words just wouldn't come out. Yet he knew if he didn't start to give Beverley more, then he would lose her. Now this. Milly, at three years old, in a state of depression about who she was. An identity crisis before she had even fully developed an identity. Despite the crisp fresh winter sunshine coming through the window, he felt a heavy weight on his shoulders.

He looked at Beverley. She really was a pretty woman. Braided hair cascading around her shoulders. Bright gleaming skin, testimony to the distance she'd kept between her face and perfumed soap. Beautiful even teeth which perfectly set off her blemish free complexion and that was just the physical part of her. She had a personality to die for. Relaxed and confident she would only get ruffled when confronted with rudeness, which was seldom. She carried herself with such confidence.

"You'll have to be careful." Beverley adjusted the curtains. Kennedy looked at his watch. He had a lot of stuff to do. On top of that it was time to take Milly to the day nursery. It was a local school with good staff. Beverley had recommended it. Her little niece, Chantelle went there and had endorsed it as only a three year old can, by crossing her legs and grinning from ear to ear. That had sold it for Beverley and Murray. Milly was equally enthusiastic when she had arrived for her first day. There were so many toys, she nearly wet herself.

"Careful about what?" That gloomy feeling was not leaving him, in fact it was getting heavier.

"Milly will be here for you whatever, but don't be sure about me."

"Beverley..."

"No, Murray," she interrupted him. It looked like she was about to elaborate on the subject, then seemed to change her mind.

"I'll take Milly this morning, give you time to think." She walked out of the room then came back a few moments later with her coat on. Milly followed behind her, traces of marmite still on her face. She had her little embroidered jacket in one hand and a relaxed looking

Mister Max in the other. She walked over to where Kennedy was standing and smiled at him.

She handed the jacket to Kennedy who smiled back and helped her put it on, first one arm then the other. The second arm was always a problem. When you were three, two arms were always something of a difficulty when putting on clothes. That's where parents came in. Kennedy gave her a kiss and held her close after he had completed the awkward task of getting his daughter into her jacket.

"Darling, you are somebody special. Never forget that." He whispered in her ear. She pulled away, an angry expression spreading across her round little face.

"No, Daddy, I've told you. I'm nobody!"

Beverley held out her hand and Milly took it. She paused as they walked out of the door and looked back at Kennedy slumped on the sofa. A slow creeping feeling of defeat spread throughout his being. She smiled briefly, over her shoulder, then they were gone.

Kennedy adjusted his position on the sofa and there was a loud squeak. He'd put his hand on Mister Max. He picked the toy up. I thought you couldn't speak. He playfully head-butted it, then to his horror saw Milly standing at the window. She'd come back and had been about to wave. There was a look of betrayal on her face as she witnessed the abuse of Mister Max. She turned and walked away.

3

Kennedy melted into the sofa. What a crap start to the day. After a while he gathered his thoughts. It was time to ring the council. The response to his letters about the sawmill barely acknowledged there was a problem. But then of course the squiggly name at the bottom of the letters didn't have to live next door to the mill. A high pitched whine told him that they'd started up again as some poor piece of rainforest was dispatched to a nether world. He sighed and picked up the phone.

A clump from the front door told him that the papers had arrived. The spotty schoolboy was always there before the postman. Postie often staggered up the path at all sorts of different times looking for all the world as though he'd been smoking crack first thing before breakfast.

Kennedy waited on the phone for a human voice to answer. He was only getting a recording and fifty different options. Press one for that, two for this and so on. He felt his patience ebbing away, but then he caught sight of Mister Max, discarded on the sofa. He was the very picture of a relaxed and cool attitude. All that Kennedy wasn't. He took a deep breath and wiggled his shoulders. That helped a little bit. After all, if a puppet could let it all pass over him, (Kennedy presumed Mister Max was a him, since he was a Mister) then surely Kennedy could.

He still hadn't reckoned with the council. By now he'd pressed the option buttons so often that his finger was hurting. Eventually a human voice answered. It sounded like a studied and composed rendering of someone who was completely interested in something other than the customer on the other end of the line.

"Good morning, how can I help you?" That was a promising start.

"Yeah, good morning. This is Mister Kennedy speaking. I'm ringing about the saw mill next to my house."

"What about it?"

This was not sounding too promising. He sighed before continuing. "I wrote to the council about the mill in our street. It's a residential area. I'm not the only person who is upset about it."

"Have you got a reference number?" The voice was impatient.

"No, what reference number?"

"If we wrote to you, there would be a reference number on top of the letter." The tone was now completely couldn't care less.

"I haven't got a number." His tone was equally unpleasant.

"So why are you phoning?" The council representative did not even try to disguise the irritation in her voice now. Kennedy had had enough.

"What's your name?"

"Why?" the voice said.

"I don't like the way you're speaking to me."

"Did I not say my name when I answered?" The tone softened, which suggested to Kennedy that there might be some kind of breakthrough.

"No, you didn't."

"So, you don't know who I am?"

"That's right," Kennedy said quietly.

"Good, then piss off!" The line went dead. Kennedy stood there for a moment looking at the receiver. He took a deep breath then slowly replaced it. He could have phoned back and made a complaint, or tried to track down the name of the woman who had been so rude, but he didn't. It would have taken half the day. Instead he walked into the hallway and picked up the paper which had landed on the floor. He scanned it briefly as he slowly went back into the front room. The headlines were all about a spiralling crime rate and the recent idea that prison officers should address inmates by their first names rather than their last. There were a few sub-headings with quotes from Joe Public about the UK going to the dogs.

There was a knock at the door. Murray put the paper down on the sofa and went into the hallway. He checked the spyhole to see who it was. You couldn't be too careful these days. Murray sighed as he opened the door. There stood Ray, well over six feet tall. His face was smooth and neat. He would have looked quite approachable were it not for his eyes which had a kind of fuck off and die look in them. And when he opened his mouth, the diamond in his front tooth merely furthered his rude boy image. His smart, designer gear probably cost more than Kennedy's fitted kitchen.

Murray smiled but he needn't have bothered. It was no secret that he was not Murray's biggest fan. Ray blinked a couple of times, and looked back at his gleaming black Lexus as though he were looking for inspiration. He was a man of few words, even fewer this morning. Flecks of sawdust danced in the air.

"Yol, Beverley!" Murray shook his head. He'd understood it to be a question.

"She's not here, she's taken Milly to the nursery." Ray looked puzzled.

"Milly?" Then recognition dawned over him just as Murray enlightened him further.

"My daughter." His tone was slightly irritated. Ray's eyes flashed as he caught the drift. Murray backed off a little bit. He was never quite sure about this guy and hero he was not.

Ray stepped back and turned to walk back to his muscle car, his leather Armani coat flapping in the breeze. He stopped as though a sudden thought had just come to mind. He turned, a little smile on his face. He looked at Murray then let his gaze drift to his stomach which was giving in to gravity. It was obviously a day of humour for Ray.

"Been to the gym, have we?" Murray stepped back and pulled in his belly drawing himself to his full height. It did not make much of an impact. Ray opened the door of the car, got in, and closed it with a satisfying thunk, the kind that seriously expensive cars make, to remind you that you are actually in a seriously expensive hunk of metal and rubber.

"Do you want to leave a message?" He shouted. Ray did not bother answering. He just reached into his coat and came out with a small cellular. Latest, state of the art, of course. He held it between finger and thumb, and dangled it out off the window.

"Right," Murray said quietly, more to himself really. He knew there were no more words coming his way from Beverley's brother. He closed the door and went back into the front room. He knew that Ray didn't like him but he could at least try to disguise it a little. Kennedy couldn't help the fact he was white. He slumped back in the sofa and threw the paper on the floor. He felt a snooze coming on. Within a short while he was fast asleep. If he'd been awake and still been reading the paper, he would have possibly come across a small item on page seven, under the overseas section. It read "Typhoon sinks ship in South China Sea. Many lives lost."

4

He would no doubt have stayed like that for hours, if the phone hadn't rung. He picked up the cordless handset by the side of the sofa and it crackled into life. He'd been meaning to replace it for ages but just hadn't got around to it. It sounded as if the Starship Enterprise was coming in to land in the earpiece. It was Maxim, phoning from Paris. Thanks to the phone he sounded as though he was attempting a re-entry into the earth's atmosphere in a go-cart. It was a while since they had spoken. Not since Murray had taken that cello from London to Milan. It was so big that it had taken up two seats in business class. He was surprised the flight attendant hadn't asked the instrument if it wanted the veggie option.

Ever since the accident ended his career as a principal violinist, Kennedy had worked for several specialist agencies based in London, Paris and New York. The agencies arranged for the safe transportation of very rare and valuable musical instruments from their owners to those who wanted to hire them for a set period of time. Clients included museums, private individuals, and many of the world's premier orchestras. All provided instruments to particular soloists for the duration of their engagement. For instance, a virtuoso may agree to play for a season only if the promoter or the orchestra in question, agrees to provide them with a particular instrument which he or she could never afford to buy or hire themselves. But of course this means getting the instrument from wherever it is in the world, to the place that the performance will actually take place, in time for rehearsals.

These pieces of art, for that is what they are considered to be, cannot be Fedexed or mailed, and they certainly can't be put in the hold of an aircraft or ship. They must be couriered by an escort who will not let the precious cargo out of their sight. It has to be in the care of an individual who would treat the instrument like a new born baby, their own in fact. Changes in temperature, pollution in a city, smoke from cigars or cigarettes can all cause damage to types of wood or the internal mechanisms of these precise and temperamental instruments. Basically, the best type of courier and the one who would be paid the most, was someone who loved music and was in love with the means of making music.

Kennedy reckoned some pieces actually talked, communicated as though they had a mind, a soul and a heart. The cargo was always a living, breathing one. If the flight crew had known they would have talked to the instruments as they would to a small child. The responsibility was unique. Millions of dollars worth of instrument didn't just need talking to, there was the issue of security. Try taking a piss with a music case under your arm which can't be put on the ground. In terms of reliability and safety a low profile individual courier was a far better bet than the security firms, who always seemed to hire the very individuals they were trying to avoid. The amount of work varied but each job was extremely well paid.

"Murray, how are you?" Maxim was a very serious and formal man but unfortunately he always sounded like a camp interior designer from Los Angeles. Murray had never told him this, Maxim lacked the British sense of humour. But then he would, he was French.

"I have a lovely one for you, Murray. A truly beautiful piece." Maxim sounded truly enthused. It must be something special for him to sound this upbeat. Murray knew that Maxim would not expand any further. He checked Murray's availability and told him the destination to and from. The final arrangements were always done face to face and Murray would be checked in under a variety of names all with bona-fide passports. The agency had a special relationship and understanding with the police and the customs officials. Maxim had made it his business, over the years, to work that front.

"How is everything, Maxim, business good?" Kennedy examined himself in the full-length mirror by the phone. The tell-tale start of a paunch was more than evident. It hurt but Ray had a point. He must start going down to the gym, he thought as he pulled his flabby stomach in. There was no time like the present. There would just be time to get a session in before Beverley returned with Milly. Eventually he let his stomach flop as he realised that he couldn't carry on a conversation and hold his breath at the same time.

"I am fine, my family are fine, all is well," the disembodied voice crackled down the line. It was never clear whether Maxim was referring to his real off-spring or the instruments which he considered as precious as any family. Before Murray could ask anymore, Maxim carried on talking, oblivious to the potential for a two-way conversation.

The job meant getting to Paris by next Wednesday and then flying out the next day to New York. A three day layover in a swanky hotel in Manhattan, would bring the whole thing to a nice rounded end. Well paid too, very well. In fact Kennedy couldn't quite remember the last time he'd picked up such a wedge for what sounded like a straightforward job. They weren't always that easy. There'd been one to Moscow. Scared the shit out of him. Post glasnost Russia made Chicago during prohibition look like Sesame Street. Although he wasn't a physical action man like Beverley's brother, Kennedy liked to think he could read situations and think on his feet, but that trip was one he wouldn't have liked to do again. A flute from the days of the revolution which looked like it still had the frost of 1917 on it. It was going to a buyer who for some unexplained reason had wanted it to be delivered to Moscow. The man who took receipt of it didn't even look Russian. Whatever, (Kennedy had never found out the proper details) the bulges in the gentlemen's jackets were definitely not music scores and they certainly didn't look like the flute playing types. Wrong type of fingers, for a start. One of them was even missing a few. Kennedy started to sweat at the memory. What was wrong with him? This wasn't the time to get nervous about his work. It brought in good money and it kept him near to the thing he loved most in his life next to Milly, music.

Kennedy confirmed the details with Maxim. He was tempted to tell him just how camp he sounded, but then thought the better of it. Maxim was his bread and butter and it wouldn't be the first time a lapse of humour resulted in someone being out of work. No thank you. Kennedy needed the money and he fancied the trip. He said goodbye, or was it au revoir, to Maxim, then examined his stomach in the mirror again.

It definitely had the two dinners look about it. That was one of Beverley's expressions for someone with a stomach which looked like they always ate two meals, their own and someone else's. He sighed deeply as he realised that fantasy was no good. The reality of the gym was the only thing which would banish the pork from his waistline. Kennedy, like so many people, had a skin which needed to sweat. It had to dispose of its stuff through his pores.

He went into the kitchen and put the dishes in the fancy dishwasher. He'd never wanted one, he actually liked washing dishes. He enjoyed the process of wetting them, turning them around, watching the water splash off at all angles. It reminded him of his childhood, which had been a happy one. His adulthood had been good too, until he lost Debbie. She'd wanted the dishwasher. They'd bought it a few days before she died. They never argued but that had been one of the few times tension had entered the relationship. She'd dragged him out to the showroom and punished him as he was forced to pretend interest in these gleaming white boxes which battered cups and saucers with a mixture of water, grit and soap.

They hadn't really talked about it. Debbie wanted the dishwasher so that's what she got. Murray had never gotten in the way of anything she wanted. He'd loved her so much, he'd basically just gone along with anything she wanted. It had meant that their relationship had not always gone smoothly as, of course, there were things he'd been unhappy about like the dishwasher. But now, the dishwasher was one of the most looked after items in the kitchen. It was a physical link with the past, with Debbie. There was Milly, their beautiful daughter, but the machine still held a ridiculous position in his affections. He couldn't put his finger on it. He breathed out heavily as he put the last of the marmite covered dishes in. Everything was covered in marmite. Milly was very thorough. Three-year-olds, like her, could give the secret service lessons in precision and application when performing certain tasks.

His memory drifted back to the rainy night in North London. It was easy to say now, but that day he'd had a bad feeling of impending doom. He'd never told anyone, they would have thought he was mad suggesting he knew that something awful was going to happen. If only they had stayed in, snuggled under the duvet, munching toast and watching the old re-runs of Top of the Pops. They'd only gone up to the supermarket to buy some things. Butter, milk and apples. The old russet variety, dark green and looking like they'd been on the ground for a while. His thoughts shot back to the present. He felt sick.

There was a big pool of powder on the floor. He'd been standing there pouring the washing machine powder into the small space where a tablet should have gone. He shook his head. What was he doing with the washing powder? That was usually kept in another room. He couldn't even remember getting it. His heart felt heavy and sad, but he didn't cry. He hadn't cried about Debbie. Even when she was laying there cold and still on the slab he hadn't cried. He'd tried to but no tears had come. He shivered at the memory. After scooping out the powder, he carefully unwrapped one of the small cubes and placed it precisely and correctly in the compartment. He used his right hand, as he did for all delicate operations. He could use his left for everyday things, like getting on a bus or picking up a bag, but not the delicate little tasks. He closed the front of the machine, checked he'd not missed anything in the kitchen, and went upstairs to his bedroom.

The violin sat in the corner of his room, gathering dust. It was covered in flight stickers from the different places he'd been. His had been a very promising career, cut short by the accident. His grip and handling of the instrument was no longer what it once was. Enough for a good musician but not enough for a world class one. If he couldn't be among the best, he had no will to play and so he'd given up.

The irony of it was that he'd defied the thugs and bullies when he was young. Despite his size, his none too gentle schoolmates would always wait to beat him up because he liked music and the violin was considered to be 'girlie'. He'd come through all that though it had left an emotional scar. It had always seemed to him that the kids who would beat up someone for playing an instrument, were just as likely to fight a child because they had a different skin colour or appeared to come from a different religion or cultural background. People would say that's kids for you. Bollocks. As far as Kennedy was concerned it wasn't about kids, it was about being nasty and cruel. Not all kids were unkind or vicious, just some, and they could learn the error of their ways.

Kennedy's whole life had been music. After school, where he had not excelled at anything except music, he went straight to college, studying everything he could about his craft. He swiftly got a chance to transfer to the Royal College of Music, where his skill had continued to improve. There were a lot of young people there, but none seemed to take much notice of class or money. Everyone was obsessed with their own paths. He smiled to himself. It could have gotten a bit chaotic at the music college if people were waiting to chase other students home, just because they played instruments other than their own.

His career leading to that of principal soloist had been a hard one. He'd always been close to his mum and dad, both of whom had passed away. No brothers or sisters meant that Debbie had been his family, his means of support. She'd been everything to him. The only saving grace after her death and the loss of the proper use of his arm, had been the opportunity to get work as a specialist courier.

Kennedy was in no doubt. If that hadn't happened, Milly or not, he would have been dead by now. The deep depression would eventually have led to his demise and there was nothing he, or anyone else could have done about it.

The squeal of the kettle told him the water was ready for his cup of tea. He'd been so engrossed in his thoughts he'd forgotten he had put the kettle on. He closed the door on the violin, the dust, and the painful memory of what might have been if Debbie had still been alive.

5

Business was good for Pai-Lan. His Gucci watch and Hugo Boss suit stood out from all the monotoned outfits of the poor. The peasants acknowledged him as he walked, head straight and back erect. How he hated them. The way they moved, the way they talked, smelling like shit all the time. Most of all he despised them for their childish dreams. Did they really think that the Five Circle Boys gave a stuff about them and their pathetic little lives? The Five Circle Boys were boss men, a powerful triad. Their role in life was to control, lead and most of all to make money.

Pai-Lan had to admit though that without their dreams these peasants inhabiting the whole of South East China would not be such easy pickings for him and his associates. He smiled innocently and gently at a young girl picking up some fruit she'd spilled from a basket. He thought she'd look good with her ankles around her ears as he gave her a good seeing to. He bent down pretending humility and picked up an apple from the ground for her. His nose wrinkled and his ardour disappeared as he smelt her peasant smell. She thanked him as he stood up and gruffly turned away to continue with his work. He and the others were scanning the town in the province of Fujian today. They would walk and mingle, deliberately dressed up to suggest wealth and success. They presented themselves as men of consequence.

Only a fool or someone tired of living would suggest that he and his compatriots were gangsters. If anyone messed with them then they would be given a

Mastermind. He smiled at the memory of the English hard man who'd given him that little morsel. A Mastermind was when someone got sorted, good and proper as they say in London. I've started so I'll finish. He laughed a little. The last he'd heard of the hardman, he'd spawned a book and hosted his own chat show. Who said crime didn't pay? Of course the chat show would only last until the producer got threatened with a bit of acid to the face. He looked around as he walked. The scum would always come to him, wringing their hands and pleading for help to make a better life for themselves and their families, in the West.

The boys would sort it out. The family would find, one way or another, the required $10,000 to form a down payment on the $30-$50,000 required for each to be smuggled to the West. Many wanted to start a new life in New York. The locals called the Big Apple "The Golden Mountain" because of all it represented—wealth and happiness. Times were especially lucrative for the Five Circle Boys now because the Asian economic crisis had really started to bite. The peasants couldn't make ends meet despite their traditional ingenuity and flexibility in producing trade goods. The great thing was that no-one would ever find the money required to pay off the boys once they actually made it to North America or Europe. They then would become virtual slaves, working off the total sum plus interest in low paid jobs, until they dropped dead of exhaustion. Most were too poor and too closely watched to let their relatives know the truth. And anyone who did manage to tell was not believed anyway. The dream and hope in the hearts of the people in China were too strong to listen to words of wisdom from those who had gone before them. People would just think that they didn't want them to join them because they wanted it all for themselves.

Pai-Lan shook his bald head at the stupidity of it all

and the astounding economics. (He had shaved his head to look stylish, though it merely made him look meaner.) Each cheap grain boat they bought and crewed with pirates and vagabonds meant an outlay of $200-300,000. But the same boat would turn an eventual profit of about $9 million. He whistled through his teeth. He could never get his shiny hairless head around that figure.

"Oi, Pai-Lan!"

The shout came from behind a group of farmers who were gathered together by a small pen which held a few scruffy, undernourished goats. It was Cody, another of the gang. No-one knew his Chinese name but he only answered to Cody. Tall, thin and with a weasel face he was obsessed with the Wild West and had adopted part of Buffalo Bill Cody's name for himself. His eyes were dead and lifeless because there was no heart for them to connect to. Even Pai-Lan felt himself shivering in his company and avoided him whenever he could. Even a psychopath like Pai-Lan had his standards.

"Big man wants to see you now."

Pai-Lan nodded and walked swiftly towards the drinking club where he knew he would find the boss. Opium smoke and the smell of sweat and rice wine hit his nostrils as he pushed his way into the club, heaving despite the fact it was mid-afternoon. Most of the clientele were Five Circle Boys or their less important associates and colleagues. There sitting in the corner with two frightened looking young girls was the Big Man. His name was not given to him by accident. He was very fat and sweaty and dressed in an immaculate Brooks Brothers suit. He smiled like a buddha and his belly wobbled as he groped one of the scared young women's breasts. Drips of sweat fell onto his tightly buttoned white shirt.

"Pai-Lan, good to see you. Have a feel." He pulled the girl's breast out of her dress. Her nipple was swollen with fear rather than excitement.

Pai-Lan puckered his lips. A single bead of sweat dripped down his forehead, despite his best attempt to appear relaxed. This was the only individual he knew who could make him feel this way. He had to humour this man. He was the leader and nothing should be done to make him lose face.

"Go on, help yourself." He spat as he sensed Pai-Lan's hesitation.

Pai-Lan knew better than to make the wrong judgement. He went down on one knee to signify respect for the big boss and at the same time reached forward and fondled the adolescent breast being offered to him. He withdrew his hand after a few moments, both to his and the girl's relief.

"What's wrong Pai-Lan? Do you prefer bigger titty?"

Pai-Lan waited a few moments trying to judge this human mongoose's mood. After a moment he nodded. The big man roared with laughter spilling his expensive German beer all over himself and his unwilling companion. The other girl sat stock still and expressionless; her heart beat wildly. She felt sorry for her friend but was grateful that she was being spared, at least for now.

"You've been spending too much time in New York. All that big titty has gone to your head." He roared again and continued, "You want to get used to some proper little Chinese titties, at least their real and not full of plastic."

He loved the word titty. Pai-Lan, however, couldn't stand it and was becoming increasingly uncomfortable. Not for the girls, he couldn't care less about them. He just wanted this very dangerous man to come to the point. The irony of Pai-Lan's distaste for the big man's crudity was lost on himself. Pai-Lan didn't do irony, like bleary-eyed adolescents don't do mornings. As though he'd read his mind, the fat one suddenly and viciously pushed both girls away, knocking one of them off the seat. She lay where she fell while the other sloped off into the darker section of the club.

His eyes narrowed, and if he'd looked drunk before then it must have been an act because the man now sitting in front of Pai-Lan was perfectly sober. "I've got a job for you. Peasant by the name of Tei-Yon. Shooting his mouth off, suggesting we're not to be trusted. Usual shit. Seems he's a bit pissed about the loss of his brother on The Happy Dancer." Big Man sniffed and laughed at the same time. "As though the weather is in our control." He looked around for a reaction. Everyone, including Pai-Lan, wisely laughed at this sarcastic joke. The big belly rumbled with pleasure at his own limitless wit.

"The grasshopper lives up by the bell. He's making too much noise in the grass. Step on him." It was an instruction, not a request. Pai-Lan nodded and finally stood up. Big man had not given him an indication that he should have risen sooner.

"Oh Pai-Lan," Big Man said as he was turning to leave.
"Yes, boss."
"I don't want to hear another noise from this rodent. You understand? I want him to join the brother he's been going on about." Pai-Lan nodded, turned, and left.

He was in the mood for this. This fool who couldn't keep his mouth shut would help Pai-Lan in his research. As a fixer he had taken out many men and women. Killing was his business. Lately though, he began to notice something odd. The victims he tortured always screamed ...eventually. There was always a way to make them. But the strange things was, and he'd never gotten used to this, that when he used his knife to kill they never made a sound. The first time he thought it was just a fluke. Now he knew that it was the norm. He couldn't sit through films now knowing that all the grunting and screaming was made up. When you took someone out with a knife they just died—end of story. Now Pai-Lan had a quest to see if someone, anyone, would eventually make a noise.

He always used the same knives. Two double-edged daggers, each with a vein running down its length, for draining the blood. He loved them. They were oriental in origin although he wasn't sure if they were Chinese, more than likely they were from Taiwan. He also had a Second World War SS dagger. (Pai-Lan was obsessed with the Nazi era.) He'd picked this one up from a specialist dealer in Antwerp on one of his European trips. Very special. His dagger held an honoured place for him because it was actually owned not by a German but by a Dane, a member of the Norland Division who defended the Reich Chancellery until the Red Army invaded Berlin towards the end of the war. The Belgium dealer had authenticated it.

He walked up the main street towards the old bell. It was the one used to call the peasants in from the fields when work was over. It was no longer used but was left to remind people of the virtues of hard work and resilience. Fools, he thought.

Pai-Lan's methods were simple but effective. He'd come to do the job now and there was no room for failure. He checked out Tei-Yon's house. Like most of the others in Fuzian it was actually quite spacious, as so many people lived under one roof. There was one door at the front and one at the back. He knew what to do. He knocked at the front door. A woman answered, probably Tei-Yon's wife. The fear was palpable on her face. Pai-Lan sniffed and made no effort to appear anything other than menacing.

"Tei-Yon. Get him, now!" He looked straight through her. She knew better than to argue and turned away closing the door behind her.

Like an oil slick Pai-Lan oozed round to the back door just before a very frightened young man came out.

"Tei-Yon, going somewhere?"

Pai-Lan stepped in front of him. There was no-one else

around. He'd made sure of that before going ahead with his plan. Tei-Yon's lips were dry with fear. He knew that his only chance of survival was to attack first. He rose onto the balls of his feet and aimed a fast hard kick with his front foot. Pai-Lan was too fast and had been expecting it. He caught the foot and swept the other so the young man fell on his back. But with one smooth movement Tei-Yon was back on his feet, whipping his body up off the ground and punching Pai-Lan in the face with a wicked right hook.

Pai-Lan reeled and lost his balance for a moment but quickly recovered. He shifted all his weight onto the balls of his feet and delivered two powerful kicks. The first lashed into Tei-Yon's midriff, snapping two ribs with a satisfying pop. Pai-Lan then swivelled on the ball of his left foot so that his foot arched high and was parallel to the ground. The Japanese call it a mawashi-geri, the Chinese called it something else, but Tei-Yon would know it as totally bad news and the beginning of the end. Too busy spitting out his teeth to defend himself, he was swept. Both feet left the ground and he landed flat on his back with his assailant looking down at him. Tei-Yon knew he was about to die. Pai-Lan let out a satisfied grunt and with one practiced movement seized one of his daggers from it's specially designed, greased leather holster strapped high on his upper arm. It was dipped in deadly nightshade. He plunged the knife into Tei-Yon's throat with such force, that the point pierced through the other side of his neck. Then with a flick of the wrist he brought the blade forward. The man died without a sound.

Pai-Lan was bitterly disappointed as he wiped the blood off the dagger with a piece of cloth he kept especially for that purpose. He frowned. Then without looking back, he walked slowly away. Tei-Yon's lifeless body lay crumpled on the ground, twisted like a puppet with no strings; his face expressionless. Pai-Lan was a good distance away by the time Tei-Yon's young wife discovered his body. He didn't hear her scream. It sounded like a dying swan.

He'd walked some distance when something caught his eye. There was a speck on his designer jacket. It couldn't be blood. Pai-Lan was too good for that. He always positioned himself so that the blood of his victim flowed away from him. He stopped and inspected it. It was a tiny fleck. Toothpaste. Shit. He's have to get rid of that electric toothbrush. All that vibration sending the stuff all over his gear. He was pissed off now. Irritation quickened his pace. He was going straight home. No need to tell the big man that the deed was done. Fuzian was a small place when it came to news travelling fast.

He stopped to regain his composure and looked out in the direction of Taiwan. The sea was choppy and brewing, like liquid in a witch's cauldron. He sniffed as he thought of The Happy Dancer going down in the typhoon. He and his mates were all safely on land that night. Not that he ever travelled on these stinking boats. If they were heading for North America he would fly first class to Vancouver to await the arrival of the boat's cargo. If they were bound for Europe then he flew to Rotterdam or one of the other feeder ports for the United Kingdom. It was a complex operation which depended on the co-operation of several different factions of the triad. The Vancouver end was crucial, it was where the illegal immigrants would start their overland journey across the border to the United States. Pai-Lan would see it started, then fly business class to meet them in New York. This time he had another job to attend to, so he would be arriving a few days ahead of them. The other item to be taken care of was tricky, but it would reap major dividends.

As for the people smuggling, so far there had been no problems. A few boats were apprehended by the Canadian authorities but that was after the people were off them. The British Columbian coastline had not been chosen by accident. The vast sprawling wilderness made it impossible to police. You only got caught by a combination of bad luck or someone shooting their mouth off. No-one he knew was that tired of living just yet. The European side of the operation was smooth enough. The borders had effectively all but disappeared. Now the only tricky bit was smuggling them onto a boat in a truck already filled with vegetables or fruit. The customs men were not fully clued in to the success of this method yet and that suited Pai-Lan and the Five Circle Boys just fine.

The wind got his attention. It was howling now and the sky had joined the sea in a dirty grey mix. He raised his eyebrows. It looked like there was more nasty weather on the way. Hardly surprising. After all, it was typhoon season. They'd picked this time to ship people out because the motivation of the Chinese authorities to be out looking for human cargo was just about nil if they thought it might be risky. Bottom line was that the only people who really cared whether these people lived or died were the profit masters of the triad.

His thoughts turned to the new dawn which he knew would come with the Little Dragon. No-one knew who the Little Dragon was. But he did. His own power would surge when the Little Dragon took control, but only when the time was right. He turned the collar of his jacket up and walked away from the swirling sea, whistling the tune to Mastermind. Somewhere far out in the filthy water, a small piece of what used to be the Happy Dancer floated on it's oil streaked surface.

6

Beverley dropped Milly off at the Wee Yins nursery. The head of the nursery was Scottish and the name had been his idea. It reminded him of his home in sunny Clydebank. She had a quick word with the staff who said that Milly was doing fine and that they hadn't noticed anything particularly wrong with her. In fact, she had been quite upbeat. They promised to keep an eye on her. Beverley said her goodbyes and walked slowly down the leafy Islington street. A steady stream of shoppers were coming in and out of the supermarket clutching their reward cards. Just another half million quid's worth of food to eat and they would qualify for a toaster. Beverley shook her head. The giant shops cut prices to above what they should be and hypnotise the punters into thinking they are saving money by spending it.

Her mobile rang and she answered, holding it gingerly to her ear. The recent programmes about cancer and radiation from the phones had unsettled her. Her mum had suffered from breast cancer. It had taken her so quickly. One minute, a big proud woman, the next they were laying her to rest in cold English soil. Some of the family had wanted to take her back to Jamaica but Beverley's mother had been unsentimental about back a yard. England had been her home all these years so to her it made sense for her to lay her bones here. So that's what they had done, a cold dark morning with a hard rain falling from the sky. The memory still made her blood run cold. If it had been up to Beverley and some other members of her family, her mother would have gone home to Jamaica to rest, but it wasn't. You have to respect the last wishes of a departed one.

It was Cordelia phoning. They'd been friends since school days and there was nothing they didn't share. Friendship didn't come much deeper.

"How goes it, girly?" Cord's deep husky tones sliced down the earpiece. If she ever wanted to change careers she could do worse than telephone chat lines. Her octave range meant she could do man or woman. In this life it pays to be versatile.

"I'm alright, darling," Beverley said as some leaves blew in front of her face. She sat down on the old iron bench, under the tree. A small brass plaque had the inscription defaced beyond recognition. There was no way of knowing to whom the seat was dedicated.

"Everything alright on the man front?" Cordelia rarely wasted time getting to the point.

"Well..." Beverley hesitated as she picked her bag up off the ground and placed it next to her on the seat. She'd just noticed all the various types of grunge on the concrete. The traffic buzzed past her on Upper Street, making it quite difficult to hear Cordelia on the other end.

"I love Murray, I really do, but I don't feel I've got his complete attention." She pushed her little bag towards the back of the bench.

"There's only one time you got a man's complete attention, sweetie." Cordelia did not like men, period. Beverley frowned as she knew what was coming next.

"When you're spread-eagle and your panties are hanging off one leg." Cordelia had a way with words.

"It's not that simple and there's more than that to Murray." Beverley could feel her hackles rising. She did not share Cordelia's blanket assessment of the male race, although she had to admit there didn't seem a problem with his concentration when she was in the position Cordelia had just described. She stopped herself thinking along that path, not wanting to turn into Cordelia.

"I just want more from him, and I feel guilty because I know everything he's been through."

"Look, I'm free just now. Do you want to meet up?" Cordelia's tone was less husky and she sounded more like the kind, generous, friend Beverley knew she was.

"Yeah, that would be nice."

"Is Errol's good for you?" Cordelia voice was breaking up as the signal grew weak. She was obviously driving. Beverley would have to speak to her. It was dangerous to do that stuff.

"Fine. In about an hour," Beverley replied as she stood and retrieved her bag from the bench.

"Bye."

Cordelia's last word was really only just a mass of static and noise. Beverley punched the end button on her mobile and flipped the lid back into place. She felt a ringing in her ear. Probably just her imagination. Anyway, there was a public telephone five trees down the street; she now used her mobile only when absolutely necessary. Once in the phone booth, she placed her bag on the ledge in front of her next to the cards advertising prostitutes. There was even one in the position which Cordelia had described. Beverley punched in Murray's number on the grubby phone.

"Yeah?" Murray still sounded distracted, but his voice was good to hear nevertheless.

"Cordelia phoned. I'm meeting up with her so I won't be around till later."

"Fine. Maxim phoned." It was good to listen to a voice which didn't have a crackle in it.

"And," Beverley waited for him to finish the sentence. "...I've got a job. Off to Paris next Wednesday." He didn't really sound pleased or unhappy about it.

"That's good, Murray. You'll get a chance to think about what I said."

There was a pause.

"I really care about you, Beverley."

She waited a beat before she spoke.

"Murray, I know that. Do you think I would be around you if I didn't think that? I don't want you to care more I want more from you. You know exactly what I mean."

"Yeah I do." His voice was quiet and clear.

"See you later, Murray." Her money was running out.

"Yeah, see you." The line went dead.

"Damn!" Murray swore quietly to himself. He'd forgotten to tell her that Ray had come calling.

Beverley retrieved her bag from beneath the cards and forced open the doors of the kiosk. Why didn't they ever build these things with doors which could be opened by mere mortals?

Beverley walked with a bright and breezy air down towards the bus stop. She felt better, she always did when she got things off her chest. She was also looking forward to seeing her 'spar' as Cordelia liked to call herself.

She didn't have long to wait. Four buses, all the same number, ground to a stop like a clumsy mechanical ballet line. Chalk Farm wasn't a long way to go and she preferred the bus to the tube. Too hemmed in and too many unhealthy people bent on spreading their poison with their one hundred and twenty five mile an hour sneezes. Why don't people cover their mouths when they sneeze?

She presented her coin and got a grunt and a ticket in return. The bus driver did not look at all happy. Why do so many people do jobs they clearly hate? Beverley thought to herself as she sat down on the slashed leather seat. Graffiti on the back of the seat in front of her reflected the profound thoughts of the Hothead Posse, whoever they may have been. Beverley probably went to school with them. She remembered her friend's husband, he was a bus driver. Hated his job, always snappy. Then he discovered himself, some born again thing. Now he was full of the joys of life and interacted with everyone. That was even more spooky. People seemed to prefer the grunting, including Beverley. It just seemed more natural and honest.

The bus lurched its way slowly through the traffic as Beverley let her thoughts wander back to Murray. She loved the man. Really did. Milly was beautiful and Beverley knew she loved the small child but that wasn't the same as having one of your own. There was something else too. Beverley felt really guilty about this, but basically she was jealous of the fact she seemed to have to compete with a memory. Murray clearly hadn't gotten over the loss of Debbie, but life demands that you eventually move on, if you are going to survive. It was just so difficult to discuss this with Murray without seeming totally selfish and hard. After all Beverley wasn't sure how she would have reacted in Murray's place.

Eventually the bus finished its awkward and clumsy journey to Chalk Farm and deposited Beverley at the stop just a few minutes walk from Errol's cafe, or brasserie as he liked to call it. This time she got a scowl instead of a grunt from the driver, as she alighted from the smelly bus.

Cordelia was already there, surrounded by bags. She was a serious shopper.

"Girl, you look fine." Cordelia stood up and embraced Beverley like the sister she never had. Her black skin, just creamed, glistened in the sunlight and her eyes danced with pleasure. She was always happy, just her way. If there were any tears, they stayed private.

"You don't look so bad yourself." Beverley returned the compliment, which was not hard. She was a seriously good looking young woman. Sound bone structure, perfect skin, and eyes which twinkled and danced like flowers in the wind.

Errol himself came over to serve them. It wasn't his real

name, no-one knew what that was. He liked it that way. When he did business, like running this brasserie, it just made sense to keep your own name to yourself. That way the only people who found you, were the ones you wanted to. Someone once said that he looked like the singer from Hot Chocolate. So since that man's name was Errol that was fine.

Beverley ordered cranberry juice and Cordelia had a coke. "Junk food queenie" was her nickname. She loved shitty food and drink. That was why it was so funny that she had a complexion which looked like she lived most of her life on a health farm.

"So what's going on?" Cordelia asked with a directness a debt collector would have admired. Beverley smiled as she took a sip of her juice which Errol had brought swiftly and with a smile, as he always did. Beverley shrugged as she swallowed the juice. It tasted nice. Errol knew how to serve the stuff properly. There was more to it than slinging a carton of juice into a glass. Chilled, stirred, and just the right thickness. There even appeared to be bits of cranberries floating about in there.

"Like I said, I want things to move on with Murray." Beverley looked at Cordelia as she happily slurped her coke. Cordelia was not one to let you guess whether she was enjoying herself or not.

"What does he say?" Cordelia asked as she sucked on the lemon which had come unstuck rather unwillingly from the side of the glass.

"Well, I've told him how I feel. He certainly seemed to hear me, but it was a bit funny today. Probably not a good time." She took another swig of her juice.

"There's never a good time for men, honey." Cordelia was not the most generous of people when it came to members of the opposite sex. She could thank a few bad experiences for that. She did not forgive easily and had a memory like a spear fisherman. They always know exactly how much air they have left before the bends await them.

Beverley raised her eyebrows. She'd forgotten just how anti-men Cordelia could be. And the fact that he was white didn't help either. "What are you up to later?" Cordelia asked.

"I'm collecting Milly."

"Milly?" Cordelia hoovered up the remainder of her coke.

"His little one."

"Oh, yeah. I remember. Sweet young thing." Cordelia gestured to Errol who had been hovering. He was good with customers. Always on hand in case they wanted something else.

"Same again?" Cordelia looked with one eye at Beverley who shook her head in refusal. Cordelia pointed at her own glass and Errol got the message.

"So, how was it left?" Beverley had Cordelia's full attention again.

"That was it, really. I told him how I felt then took Milly to the day nursery." Beverley checked her watch. It wouldn't be that long before she picked her up again.

They chatted for a while about mutual friends, sport, sex and shopping. They covered all the usual suspects. Eventually it was time for Beverley to leave. She had a few things to do before she collected Milly from the family centre. She stood up and kissed Beverley on both cheeks.

"Don't forget, darling." Cordelia was looking for her purse as she spoke.

"Forget what?" Beverley waved goodbye to Errol who nodded back with a smile.

"To hook him right." Cordelia smiled like a big game hunter.

"He's not a fish." Beverley gave her a wry look as she walked away from the front of the brasserie.

"Babe?" Cordelia shouted after her.

"Yeah?" Beverley was now some distance away.

"They're all fishes, except the ones who're dogs." Cordelia was laughing as she shouted and toasted Beverley with her glass of coke.

Beverley waved her hand dismissively as she got into her stride. A bus was pulling alongside the stop just as she got to it. This bus driver was pleasant. At least there's one, thought Beverley as she got on and paid her fare. Just as the bus pulled off her mobile rang. A few other people on the bus reached for theirs. There were few ring tones left. She smiled at the self-conscious faces as they realised that the phone ringing was not theirs.

"Hello Sweetie." It could only be one person. No-one except her brother called her that.

"Ray. Where ya been?" She put on a mock scolding accent. It was really good to hear from him. She settled down in a seat next to a large bald man who obviously did not have deodourant in his vocabulary or his shopping bag. Beverley pushed herself in a bit forcing him to close his legs. She hated guys who sat on the bus with their legs wide open leaving precious little space for anyone else. He did not react. Wise.

"Where are you, sis?"

"On the bus heading back to Murray's."

"Yeah, right." The tone told her all she needed to know and all that she already knew. Ray would quite obviously have preferred her to have a black girlfriend than a white boyfriend, but there was something particular about Murray which he seemed to have taken a real dislike to. She hadn't gotten to the bottom of it yet.

"I called round there this morning," he continued. "He said you'd taken his kid to the nursery."

Strange. Murray hadn't said that he'd phoned.

"Get off at the stop near the cinema on Seven Sisters Road and I'll meet you there, sis. I've got a few minutes and we can have a chat," Ray said.

Beverley laughed. "Thanks for fitting me in."

"You're welcome."

The irony was a bit lost on Ray. He was straight up. Didn't do sarcasm very well. It wasn't his style. He was parked in the section in front of the bus stop. He shouldn't have been there, it being a red route and all. The bus driver cursed as he had to stop further out than he would have liked. He opened his door to say something to the driver of the gleaming Lexus but when the window purred down he saw Ray. He changed his mind and just mumbled something as Beverley got off the bus.

Beverley got in the back seat. Misjudging the smoothness of the leather, she slid right across barely managing to hang onto her shopping. The front seat was occupied by a huge man who made the massive proportions of the Lexus seem modest by comparison. He turned round as Ray gunned the motor and eased into the traffic flow. He smiled at Beverley. It was a supposed to be a warm welcoming one, but it wasn't. The two eyes looked like something from a deep sea predator. There may have been a neck, once in his younger days, but now his head seemed to be connected directly to his body. Add the pock-marked skin and it meant that whatever Ray's spar spent his time doing did not involve fashion modelling on the catwalks of Milan. The head sniffed.

"Whatcha, Bev." The voice was hard and grated like a month old cheese.

"You alright, Lex?" Whatever else he was this man had a burning loyalty to Ray and there was nothing he wouldn't do for him.

"Good to see ya, sis." Ray flashed a smile at Beverley as he drove past Pentonville Prison, a place Ray had somehow managed to stay out of, just. Lex hadn't been so lucky, he had less than rosy memories from that place. Alright he was a crim but he had his morals and some of the things which went on in there just weren't right. Ray waved his right hand, the one carat diamond glinting as he did so.

"I'll take ya home, alright?"

"No, take me to the nursery, I"m picking Milly up."

Ray frowned. "Can he not do it?"

"Not that it's any of your business, but no. Anyway, I want to do it."

She leaned forward, resting her chin on the back of his seat. She was careful not to move too fast, as she now realised that the leather had no friction on it. Lex was busy checking out the honeys and kept a respectful silence. Years ago he learned not to get involved in family stuff. Once, some irate brother had taken exception to his opinion about his sister. He had tried to take his eye out with a kitchen knife. Unfortunately, Lex had been forced to break his arm and fracture his jaw to ensure his own safety. Never interfered with families since. He rubbed his pock-marked chin and wondered whatever had happened to Crystal. She was fit alright. Not surprisingly the relationship had taken a downward turn after Lex had introduced her brother to Accident and Emergency. He frowned at the memory. It was a while before the guy was able to eat solids again. Beverley directed Ray to the nursery as Lex kept his attention on the pedestrians flashing past the car window.

"What do you want, Ray?" Beverley's tone was a bit sharp. Ray's disapproval of her boyfriend was beginning to wear a bit thin.

"Why do I have to want anything. Can't I just come and see my favourite sister, when I want?" He sounded a bit hurt. He slowed up as they were nearly at the nursery.

"Yeah, whatever." Beverly wasn't convinced.

Ray had brought the Lexus to a complete standstill. Children were coming out of the nursery with excited little whoops of joy, delighted to be scooped up by their waiting parents or big sisters.

He turned round to look at her. "It's just I want the best for you, sis. I don't feel the guy's right for you."

"Cos he's white?"

"Yeah, but not just that. He's just too...soft."

"So, what do you suggest? Hard? Like some of your bredrin. Walk round with a face like a bag of spuds, from too many beatings. No thanks."

Lex turned round at this. He looked a bit hurt as though Beverley's comment had been directed at him. He'd only ever hit a woman once, or maybe it was twice. He couldn't be sure. Wasn't his fault some of the girls turned out to have a few marbles loose. He'd only ever slapped them around to protect himself. They'd usually come at him without any warning, unless you call screeching down the phone advance notice of an impending attack. Beverley held his gaze. She wasn't in the mood to back down. There was a short tense silence, broken by the sound of the car door closing. Beverley had gotten out of the vehicle. She walked round to the driver's side and bent down so that her face was level with Ray's.

"I know you care. But some things just aren't any of your business. I don't tell you who you can see."

Ray looked straight ahead. Experience had told him that Beverley always got the better of a shouting match, besides it was bad form to be seen shouting at a woman in public. That may be alright for some of the rude bwoys, but Ray considered himself to have more class than that and he didn't want to end the conversation on a bad note. After all he'd come to give his baby sister a birthday present. She'd always meant a lot to him, even more so now Mummy was gone, snatched before her time by the big C.

"How's Rex?" he asked quietly, puncturing the tension and reminding Beverley that he cared.

She smiled her unique smile. "He's fine. Very big though."

"That's the whole idea, isn't it? What's the point of having a small Rotweiler? It wouldn't have much impact then, would it?"

"Nah, I suppose not."

"I nearly forgot." Ray reached across into the glove compartment, brushing against Lex as he did so. He was a big lad. He held out a little brightly wrapped package to Beverley.

"What's this?" she asked.

"Your birthday. You thought I forgot, didn't you?"

"Well, it was two weeks ago."

"Been busy."

She unwrapped it to find a small highly polished brooch fashioned into the shape of a bird.

"It's a Canadian goose. Flies south in the winter, just like you." He smiled and touched her hand.

"Thanks, Ray. It's really nice, honest." She pinned it to her chest. He knew how much she liked anything to do with birds.

He smiled and started the motor. A little squeal behind her told her that Milly had joined them. She turned and gathered the little girl up in her arms. Ray pressed the gas gently and moved off.

"See you, sis."

Lex had his arm out of the window stroking the paintwork of the smooth paintwork. The gleaming gold Rolex Daytona on his wrist seemed to smile at him. At least that's the way it seemed to him. He loved Rolex watches, that was why his homies gave him that nickname.

Ray turned to Lex. "Train?"

Lex nodded. "Let's do it, bredrin."

Milly seemed happy enough. The staff of the nursery stood at the gate. They always saw the little ones off. They said that she hadn't said anything which resembled the stuff she'd gone on about before, being nobody. All very

43

strange.

"What's that?" Milly pointed at the brooch.

"A goose. It's a present from Ray, for my birthday."

"What's a goose?"

"A kind of bird." Beverley tucked back a few of Milly's stray curls.

"Oh."

"Come on, we've got some shopping to do before we go home." She took Milly by the hand.

7

Murray was waiting for them when they got back. Beverley was laden with far more than she had intended to buy. If she'd known just how much, she would have gotten Ray to give them a lift. Murray looked good and there was a tingle to his skin. No need to ask where he'd been. It was always obvious when he'd worked out, he looked fresh and vital. It had been a good session but spoiled by the fact that Ray and Lex had been there doing their Karate. Murray was already feeling self-conscious because it had looked as though he had gone to the gym as a direct result of Ray's visit (which he had).

Murray gave Milly a big hug, she seemed bouncy and happy and full of what she had done at her little nursery that day. She repeated what Murray had hoped not to hear again, that she was a nobody. He wasn't sure how to deal with this. Beverley seemed to have more of a handle on it than him. Maybe it was just a woman's touch, he wasn't sure.

"So when is it you're away again?" Beverley touched his cheek tenderly. She certainly wanted more from him but deep in her heart she really wanted this to work out between them.

"Wednesday. Maxim didn't say much about it." He smiled back at her.

The timing could have been better. He had a feeling that it was not a good time to be away from her. It was as though she had read his thoughts.

"He never says much though, does he? Seems safer that way. Probably good for you to be on a trip. It'll give you time to think about us." She smiled back.

None of this was meant to be full of conflict. She loved the man for Christ's sake. But there was something else which needed clearing up.

"Murray."

"Yeah?" he rubbed his back. Overdid the gym a bit.

"Why didn't you tell me my brother called round?" Murray coloured a bit. He always went a bit red when he was caught out over something.

"I'm sorry I forgot," he said.

"You sure?"

"What do you mean?" His tone was hurt. He hadn't expected this.

"Well, you don't usually forget something like this. Have you got a problem with Ray?"

"I would have said it was the other way round. Wouldn't you?"

"Well you know where you stand with Ray. He's up front and honest."

"You can say that again. He'll let you know before he lands one on you."

"Murray!"

She resented the inference that Ray was some kind of gangster. But inside there was a small part of her that knew it was true. He was about to say something more but she stopped him with a finger to his lips. It was a habit of hers which he actually found quite endearing.

Wednesday came around very quickly. Murray managed to get a few more sessions in at the gym just down the road, after making sure there was no sign of Ray or Lex. He liked it, it was quite dirty and not at all posy. Reminded him of the old gyms when boxing was at its height in the seventies. Spit and sawdust and honest hard men came to work off their frustrations and (in most cases) hopeless dreams in a pool of salty sweat. He'd joined a few really expensive Water and Light health centres but the only thing which got lighter was his wallet. They were full of the types of people he spent most of his time trying to avoid. They always looked at their happiest when the equipment wasn't working so they could sit there posing in the bar which was really all they wanted to do in the first place. But in truth, they came from the same type of background as Murray and that unsettled him. He could rarely force himself to go.

He felt good and ready for the work; he would have to leave today. As usual, Maxim had paid for the plane ticket to Paris and there would be a car waiting for him at the other end of his journey. He'd gotten up early that morning, washed, shaved and then covered himself in a nice smelling body butter. Beverley's idea, she said most white men didn't cream their skin enough. If she was sharing his bed, never mind his life, then at the very least she expected him to look after his skin. He'd been reluctant at first but he was glad he took the advice. His skin felt good which meant he felt good. Nice and simple equation. Some loafers and casual trousers finished off the package. No jeans. Kennedy hadn't felt comfortable in them for a while so he'd thrown them away in disgust. No more Next catalogue for him. It wasn't the weight, he didn't know what it was. Probably just getting older.

The sound of a car horn told him the cab was here. Beverley and Milly were lined up like a farewell committee. Milly whispered in his ear as he bent down to kiss her.

"Daddy, I... "

He interrupted her. "Yes, Darling I know what you are. You told me already. We'll see about that."

"No daddy..." She looked surprised before she continued, "I was going to say I forgive you for beating up

Mister Max, but I'm not sure he does." Her little face was stern and resolute.

Beverley smiled and hugged him close. "Have a good trip." She kissed him lightly on the lips. He went to hold her closer but she pushed him playfully away.

"You car's waiting, sir." She guided him out of the door as he checked that he had his wallet, passport and credit cards—the most important things which he couldn't do without. Clothes and all the rest, could be bought if needed. Maxim provided a generous expense account so long as it wasn't abused, then he got kind of French about these things. This trip was probably going to be quite short so that wasn't really a worry. He also checked that he had his mobile. It was nestled in a little outside pocket of his Samsonite travel bag.

A last goodbye to Milly and Beverley and then he settled into the Mercedes. A smiling young driver turned to look at him. "It's Heathrow innit, mate? I mean, sir." He was freshly shaved with glistening teeth. Looked more like a male model than a cabbie.

"Mate's fine." Kennedy smiled back at the confident unblemished face peering back at him.

"Going far?" The young man sniffed as he checked his mirror, indicated, pulled out, and looked at Kennedy in the mirror. All one manoeuvre. It didn't stop him narrowly missing an estate car.

"Blimey, where did he come from?" He shifted position in his seat making sure he didn't crease his expensive shirt.

"So where are you going?" the driver repeated.

"Paris," Kennedy replied as he checked his luggage once more for anything he may have forgotten. Time and again he left behind something crucial to his trip.

"Paris. Went there myself once. Lovely city .... on a modelling trip," unblemished face said. Kennedy looked up and whistled softly to himself.

Heathrow took a while to get to, the M4 was always a challenge. Upon arrival Kennedy paid the driver and promised that he would indeed keep an eye out for the Häagen Dazs poster which had Kev's legs in them. Kev was not the name he used for the modelling work. He modelled under the name of Paul St Germain. Sounded more like a porn actor. Kennedy was in a reasonable mood though, so didn't say that, just thought it. Judging by the cheeky grin Kev gave him as he drove away with his fistful of money, he would probably have taken it as a compliment.

After he'd checked in for the Paris flight he grabbed himself a cup of coffee. He usually drank tea, which was better for him; he'd been turned onto the herbal stuff by Beverley. But today, he felt daring. The coffee was strong, dark and sweet, just like Beverley. He always told her that when he could remember and when he could get the timing right. The right words at the wrong time can have disastrous consequences and sometimes Kennedy needed to remind himself of that.

Overhead the long tubes of metal with their precious human contents swept over the terminal, Another coffee. Kennedy really did like tea, but somehow it felt like a coffee kind of day.

8

Thousands of miles away in South East China another cargo was being prepared for the journey to British Columbia. The down payments had been made and the two hundred and fifty souls were being led down into the dark, stinking hole which would be their home presuming they were luckier than those who floated miles beneath them on the murky ocean bed. Pai-Lan was in charge of the details for this one. He watched as they filed onto the ship. Nothing about them touched him, they might have been cattle as far as he was concerned but cattle smelt better he thought as he held a soft silk handkerchief to his nose. A minor discomfort in view of the fact that this was going to be a lucrative money-spinner. It would be good to make some cash after the financial loss they suffered from the sinking of the Happy Dancer. Things could only get better from here. As well as the North American connection, trade was picking up for the route into the United Kingdom, via Europe. Since the stupid Europricks had dropped their internal border, smuggling people to the French ports was as easy as taking rice off a dysentery stricken peasant.

At well over six foot, it was not unreasonable that Kennedy asked for an aisle seat. Even though he was flying business class, a seat by the window still meant he was just a bit too cramped. A pretty young woman resembling someone from Breakfast at Tiffany's, looked at her computer screen and was able to oblige him. Even nicer, was that she looked like she gave a damn. He took his boarding pass, his ticket and passport and went through security.

He smiled as he was frisked. Couldn't help thinking about Diana Ross and her response to being body searched when a Concorde was waiting impatiently on the tarmac for her. If Kennedy got the facts straight the Diva had objected to having her body touched by a stranger. Her response on this occasion was to touch the security guard in the same fashion. It did not bring about a favourable conclusion to the whole episode. In a fanfare of pomp and ceremony which would have done a public relations firm proud, she was led off to be interviewed by the South East's finest. She missed her flight. A Concorde waited for no-one.

The man nodded Kennedy through, the handheld machine he played over his body gave no sign of there being anything wrong. Kennedy was tempted to say something smart but thought better of it. You could get yourself into serious trouble by having a joke when you're about to board a plane. He re-adjusted his jacket and was about to pick up his luggage which had gone through the x-ray machine when the girl opposite him looked him straight in the eye. Her name badge identified her as a Ms. Maureen Jones.

"This bag belong to you, sir?" She did not smile but was politeness personified. She looked like she was of Asian origin despite the Anglo-Saxon name.

"Yes." Kennedy tried not to look impatient, but did not really succeed. Beverley had told him once, quite accurately, that he had a glass face. You could tell what he was thinking just by looking at him.

Maureen Jones started to unpack the bag as she rather coldly said,"You don't mind if I have a look inside, do you?"

She'd already opened it so the answer seemed

irrelevant. She was telling him; she wasn't asking. She pulled out his jockey shorts and freshly ironed and neatly folded shirts, unfolding them as she did so.

He couldn't help himself. It was out before he could stop it.

"Do you have to?" His tone was impatient and surly.

"The regulations state that we have the right to search any luggage we want to."

Kennedy was led into a small room to face an unsmiling supervisor. He had a slight stubble on his fleshy face where it met his collar. (Kennedy was surprised, he thought a supervisor shouldn't have stubble.) His flight was boarding, and he was stuck in a little room being inspected by Ms. Maureen Jones' uniformed supervisor, behind whom she stood sharply to attention like a new recruit. Kennedy knew that he had to behave himself if he was going to get to Paris. Must be on edge a bit. The rude response was unlike him, particularly under the circumstances. The irritation was normal but he usually managed to keep it in check.

"Let's go over this again, shall we Mister Kennedy?" The accent was middle England, it had the concrete cows of Milton Keynes stamped all over it. Super was thumbing through Kennedy's passport. It was pretty obvious it had been thumbed through many a time before. Jones was standing stock still. Kennedy pursed his lips. He had to be careful.

"I already said I was sorry. I mean it." The second bit was really a lie, he didn't meant it at all. He was only sorry because of the impact this was having on him. The supervisor did not look impressed. He fiddled with the collar of his uniform jacket. Kennedy could not make out what the uniform exactly represented. Who did he work for? It was never really clear who these damned officials actually represented.

"I wasn't questioning the right to go through my

luggage. It was the messing up of my gear. It just seemed a bit much."

"So you thought it appropriate to say what you said?" The man did not look impressed. His skin seemed to get shinier under the strip lighting. Kennedy didn't answer.

"Did you hear me, Mister Kennedy?" he demanded with authority.

"Look, I was getting a bit irate. I shouldn't have said it." Kennedy meant that bit.

"Ah, yes I think we're all agreed on that. 'Fuck the regulations' is not something which we are used to hearing." He seemed to be smiling now, which suggested that it may go Kennedy's way.

The supervisor looked at Miss Jones. She was not smiling but her impressive chest was heaving with what appeared to be anger. "In this circumstance, I have decided not to proceed further Mister Kennedy. But be warned, I could have been far less lenient."

Kennedy nodded gratefully. If he hurried he could catch his flight. He reached forward with his left hand to retrieve his belongings. The injury which would never heal, was obvious as his shirt rode up his arm. The puckered and discoloured skin a testament to the night his career as a top flight musician ended. The man whistled in sympathy, his concern seemed genuine.

"What happened there?" The supervisor asked.

"It used to be an arm," Kennedy answered. All trace of sarcasm was gone, after all it had gotten him into enough trouble for one day. Anyway, the man seemed alright.

"Still looks like an arm to me," he said gently.

Kennedy whistled through his teeth. "It's not much use for what I used to do." He gathered his belongings.

"What was that?" the supervisor asked. He was genuinely interested.

"A professional musician." Kennedy now had his bag

in front of him. If it appeared defensive, it was meant to, that was how he felt. He didn't like talking about it.

"What instrument did you play?" His eyes lit up with enthusiasm as he folded his arms and relaxed, leaning his backside against his desk.

"Violin. I was good." He hesitated then added, "Very good, one of the best." Kennedy could feel himself tensing up before adding.

"I don't play anymore. Not since this happened." He fixed the supervisor with one of his steely stares. They were unsettling at the best of times, and the worst.

"Must be a big loss." The sympathy was clear in the airport official's eyes. Kennedy walked slowly to the door, half facing the man before he paused.

"I lost a lot more than that." He eyes were rock hard, but inside he instantly regretted saying it. Why should this complete stranger give a stuff about the faultlines in my life?

He looked at the door before looking back. "Do you mind? I'll miss my flight."

The supervisor nodded, then said just as Kennedy was walking out, "Oh Mister Kennedy, one thing..."

"Yeah?" He licked his lips. Maybe his departure was not going to be so easy.

"Little more polite next time if you don't mind. My colleague was just doing her job."

Kennedy nodded then closed the door behind him. The supervisor rubbed his hands together then walked over to where Miss Jones was perched next to the kettle.

"Two sugars, please." He smiled at her. She looked back at him with a look as cold as a witch's tit. Then she put the kettle on.

Kennedy settled back in his seat on the 767 and looked out of the window as the heavy plane taxied to its waiting point on the runway. He had just made it. He didn't know what was wrong with him. He was feeling particularly low and sensitive. The sarcasm with the woman at security was silly. It shouldn't have happened. If he'd missed his flight and Maxim had found out why, it could have cost him this job. He shook his head at his own stupidity as the flight attendant walked past checking that he and his fellow passengers were all belted up. They had done the safety chat already. Kennedy paid particular attention this time. He didn't like flying and the recent spate of crashes had done nothing for his courage.

His mind was unsettled as the plane's Rolls Royce engines cranked up their power and the plane began it's take-off roll. A friend had suggested that the next time he flew he should sit in the section of the plane where they kept the flight data recorders, the black box. They always seemed to survive a crash and everyone did their level best to find them. He had a point.

Murray felt himself pinned to his seat as the giant metal beast left the ground and thrust itself through the clouds. There was some turbulence as it streaked upwards. Shit, he hated this. The advertisements said flying was safe, comfortable, glamourous and good for you. No. As far as he was concerned it was very unsafe, extremely uncomfortable, bloody unglamorous and totally shitted your system up.

Once the fasten seat belt sign had gone off, the flight attendants started to serve the drinks. Why the sign had gone off was beyond him, the plane was twisting all over the place. The trolley dollys' still had their fixed smiles in place. He didn't think that Maxim fully realised just how much he loathed flying. To be honest, it had a gotten a lot worse since Debbie's death. It had to do with a fear of being out of control, having a more fatalistic attitude, and the reality that he was the only parent left for Milly. He accepted his coke with ice and lemon (no alcohol when he flew) and looked out of the window. Memories of his Debbie flooded his subconscious. The pain was almost unbearable.

Raoul, one of Maxim's drivers, was at the airport to greet him. The resemblance to an English Lord was uncanny. Raoul always dressed impeccably and his neatly coiffured hair and manicured hands did nothing to puncture the illusion of wealth and breeding. Kennedy didn't actually know anything about his background, but it definitely wasn't Eton. They knew each other, so it wasn't necessary for Raoul to hold one of those ridiculous signs—to stand there looking like a trackside bookie on a wet afternoon in Epsom. Kennedy liked him. He knew when to talk and he knew when to shut up. Today was a shut up day and Raoul obliged. Kennedy looked at the beauty of Paris flashing past him as the smooth Citroen glided through the lunchtime traffic.

Maxim's place was tucked away in a quiet little street off the Rue de Madeleine. It was a mecca for anyone who knew what they were talking about in relation to classical instruments. In fact quite a few who didn't know what they were talking about also hung out there.

The small rotund figure of Maxim was waiting to greet him as the car came quietly to a standstill. Raoul had telephoned ahead to say that they were about to arrive. It was good to see the little Frenchman. He was an employer but Kennedy also considered him a friend. He had a small cheese in his pocket which got squashed as he hugged Kennedy. Maxim liked his cheese. There was a small trace of it still in his precise little moustache nestled above a pair of thin tight lips housing a tongue so sharp it could take a grown man to his knees with one or two well-chosen phrases. Kennedy knew. He'd been on the receiving end. Piercing blue eyes merely added to Maxim's intimidating looks.

"Hello and welcome, my friend." He guided Kennedy

in as Raoul brought in the single piece of luggage behind them. The sign announcing that it was Maxim's place looked like it could do with a clean. The pollution of Paris seemed to be catching up with that of London.

Maxim offered him some tea, but Kennedy refused. He wasn't in the mood to eat or drink just now, besides he was curious to see what he would be taking to New York.

As if he sensed Kennedy's anticipation, Maxim led him down the stairs to his working area, which housed his office. The place was wall to wall with instruments of all kinds. He was classed as a musical shop but most of his business was in the courier scene. He'd put a strongroom in some time ago when a client had voiced concern that a cello worth hundreds of thousands of dollars was going to spend the night in a room with Maxim's cheeses. He'd argued that it was the last place thieves would look if they broke in. But the clients were having none of it so Maxim had to move with the times. That had been years ago. As some of the pieces were now valued in the millions, it turned out to be a very wise move.

To the owners, the instruments were like their children. Kennedy could identify with this. It was very hard to put into words just how an instrument could grab you and hold you in its spell. Some got you in the eye, others in the heart. Some even got under your skin and yes, some actually got you in the groin.

Maxim flicked a few switches to the door of his strongroom and waited a minute for the technology to kick in. Strategically, Maxim always shielded the front of the safe with his body, so Kennedy was clueless as to the procedure. Just as well he had no interest. Light from the street above leaked into the basement. The dust played in it like a thousand angels as Maxim turned around with the flight case in hand. Clearly it was a violin, but when he opened it Kennedy gasped. It wasn't just a violin. It was an Amati! Kennedy had never actually seen one up close before. Until now, magazine photographs and paintings were his only images. He leaned forward and reached for it instinctively. Despite his understanding of such exquisite pieces of art, he forgot himself. He had been about to touch it. Like a headmaster admonishing an over-eager schoolboy, Maxim raised his hand. Kennedy expected a blow that never came.

"Sorry." Kennedy shrugged his shoulders and looked sheepish. He could not, however, tear his eyes away from the varnished wood. It was not shiny as such, nor was it spotless. There was just something about it. It hummed, and seemed as though it was alive. The grain flowed like a river and the neck resembled that of an ancient Egyptian cat. The line and proportion of the violin was stunning. It spoke to him and seemed to touch his very being. Kennedy was aware of a small blob of moisture on his shirt, he'd actually been drooling.

"It's an Amati," Maxim said slowly and deliberately. "It's come straight from Milan. It was on loan there for a while. It's owned by a lady in England." He licked his lips. "Of course, you already knew that."

He looked sideways at Kennedy who could only nod his head in agreement. He could not find any words. His throat was dry and his heart was pumping. He felt as though he was going to come in his pants. Maxim looked like he already had. More than anything else in the world he wanted to touch, hold, and indeed fondle that lump of wood and string. He reached again for it, forgetting himself. Maxim was not angry. He understood what was happening. It had been the same for him when the violin had first come in. He could not help himself either. There was something magical, something alive about it. It just grabbed you in a place you couldn't help responding to.

He gently placed his hand upon Kennedy's and gestured to the soft kid gloves by the side. Kennedy took a deep breath and smiled. "Of course. I am so sorry."

Designed for holding fine objects, the gloves made sure that no oil or grease from human skin got onto an instrument. Sweat was one of the worst things which could discolour or even warp the wood of such a violin. When it was first made in the eighteenth century people's diets were different and there were less toxins in the skin. People now were capable of letting a whole range of chemicals out through their skin, all could inflict terrible damage on an instrument.

It was amazing that there wasn't a safer way of transporting precious instruments than Maxim's operation. The simple truth was that any publicity or fancy security would alert the specialist criminals that such a rare item was on the move. No. Trust and a small band of loyal workers were the key to Maxim's success. Workers like Kennedy, who knew the value of discretion and reliability.

Now gloved, Kennedy returned to the table which supported the delicate item of their adulation. The gloves were slightly too small, they were Maxim's own—an indication of how this violin had affected him. He never allowed anyone to wear his special gloves but at this moment Maxim did not seem to care. His only thought was that no naked hand would touch his charge. It was a spiritual icon, an icon which should not be tarnished.

"Do you know how many violins like this were made?" Maxim's voice was barely a whisper and he spoke as though the instrument was a sleeping baby that he didn't want to awaken.

Kennedy shook his head no. He had a pretty good idea, but he wasn't sure. Anyway, Maxim liked his thunder and he didn't want to steal it.

"Six." Maxim said the number like a mantra. Kennedy half expected to hear a chant or the beat of a buddhist drum in the background. Maxim gestured to Kennedy that he could touch it, as he'd noted that the gloves were in place.

Even through the material of the gloves Kennedy could feel the smoothness of the wood. It was almost singing out to him. The strings looked like they were part of the instrument instead of things which were attached. He shook his head in wonder.

"It is one of the most ... beautiful things I've ever seen." His eyes were fixed on it. He could not tear them away. Without warning Maxim thrust a bow under his nose. "Play, Murray. Go on." He fixed Kennedy with a look which seemed to burrow its way right through to his heart.

Kennedy was taken aback. Maxim had never done anything like this before. "No, Maxim. It's good of you, but no." He smiled at the old Frenchman.

"Go on," Maxim said before continuing like a conspirator. "I will not tell anyone." He winked.

Kennedy's tone was hard and tense, "I said no."

He breathed deeply and evenly looking Maxim straight in the eye. Maxim pursed his lips and said nothing as he slowly put the bow away.

This all felt quite strange. Maxim was trying to help Kennedy, something he'd never done before, but it seemed to have gone horribly wrong.

Kennedy pulled the gloves off and placed them more deliberately than necessary back on the desk they'd come from. He walked a few paces then turned to face Maxim. His face had a faint streak of sweat on it. He started to speak.

"Maxim..." His employer interrupted him with a quiet but firm tone.

"It's alright, Murray. Let's discuss the details of your trip and your companion." He pointed to the violin with the same hand which had just held the bow. A first class ticket to New York's John F. Kennedy airport and two nights in the Waldorf Astoria were in the package.

Kennedy frowned when he saw the itinerary in front of him.

"Something wrong?" Maxim sniffed. Kennedy sighed and looked at the light which was still streaming through the window, but dimmer now as it was getting later.

He fingered the paper which had the details written on it in fine handwriting. Maxim paid much attention to his form, whether he was playing music, composing it, baking a cake or, indeed, writing a letter. It was one of the most attractive and irritating things about him. His attention to small precise things.

"It's the Waldorf. I'm not keen on it. I thought you knew that." Kennedy spoke quietly, for no other reason than he was tired, he could feel his eyelids dropping a bit.

"I'm supposed to remember every little detail?" Maxim spewed as he slapped the papers into Kennedy's hand.

"You usually do. Look I prefer the Royalton. It's more..."

Maxim interrupted him, "...rock and roll?" He smiled then gave a little laugh.

"Yeah, Maxim, more rock and roll." He smiled back.

That was the last clear image Kennedy remembered before falling fast asleep, covered in fresh clean linen at the hotel around the corner. The whole world could have exploded and he wouldn't have woken up. He slept right through the night. Something he hadn't done in months, probably years, since the awful night.

9

The next morning he woke up to a quick breakfast of herbal tea and two fresh croissant. Then it was a brisk walk back to Maxim's where the violin was waiting for him. Raoul was perched by the side of the motor. His hair was gelled and combed and his blue blazer was spotless with shiny gold buttons, like it had come straight from the Carlton Club. He looked like he hadn't moved since yesterday. Probably hadn't for all Kennedy knew.

"Morning," Kennedy said politely as he passed the driver and headed into Maxim's. Raoul nodded and stamped out his cigarette with the heel of his shoe. Kennedy always thought he looked like an extra from one of those sixties films featuring Corsican gangsters with the pencil thin moustaches and the blueblood eyebrows. A few pleasantries were exchanged and then Kennedy was on his way to Charles de Gaulle with a priceless violin, a few hundred dollars and a couple of croissant reforming in his stomach.

He settled back in the deep seats of the Citroen as it sped to the airport. The whole trip seemed simple enough, apart from his precious cargo. That was something else. The Amati was owned by a recluse. Her late husband inherited it through his family. Must have been well off as it was not the kind of thing you found in an old attic. There were only six ever made. Four were destroyed through the years, all documented and accounted for. The only other known one was owned by an oil magnate who lived in the Seychelles and never let it out of his sight. Probably had it surrounded by armed guards and air filters. A sad end for an instrument which after all, was made to be played. If you wanted an Amati, you had to go through Maxim who would book it with the owner. A proper fee was charged, as the owner wanted it being played only by those who really appreciated its value.

This time the client was the New York City Symphony. They had booked it for a three month run, on behalf of a maestro violin player who would only agree to the booking if he could play that instrument. In this case, Kennedy was pretty sure that Maxim had bumped the price up. But after all, he was a business, and he was French.

Raoul dropped him off at international departures. He didn't get out of the car, but flicked the boot switch from inside. That was a bit strange as Raoul usually got out to help with his bags. In fact he'd seemed a bit strange all the way to the airport. Kennedy thought no more of it as he picked up his suitcase, making sure that the case containing the violin did not touch the ground. He gave one last look at Raoul as he disappeared amongst a flurry of Citroens. Good thing about the French, they always supported their own industries. The Brits could learn a thing or two from them on that front, he thought as he walked into the terminal building.

Charles de Gaulle airport was no different than the countless others he had been in all over the world. The violin did not leave his sight, nor his side. The case had a little strap which could be placed around his body when he needed to take a piss, which was quite often, because Kennedy liked his tea and coffee. The complicated papers were always prepared by Maxim and meant there were never problems at departure and no stoppages in the U.S. Maxim always discussed the journey with the carriers beforehand although he was careful about letting anyone know the true value of the instruments concerned. You had to be careful about letting too many people know about these trips.

Kennedy put some money in a payphone. There was just enough time to ring Beverley before he had to board his plane. Everything was going smoothly and he felt like talking to her. After all, she and Milly were always in his thoughts.

He heard his own voice before Beverley picked the phone up and cut through the answering machine. "Yeah?" She sounded sweet and Kennedy felt a familiar rustle in his trousers when he heard her speak. That was good, his dislike of flying hadn't affected his libido. He looked down to make sure it wasn't too obvious, after all he didn't want to offend anyone. He was fine though, it was only a semi.

"Hi Darling, it's me." He felt his voice go a bit husky.

"You sound like you're in the mood for something special." Beverley was a woman. She always knew what a man was thinking.

He laughed. "I thought you might have mistaken me for someone else." A flurry of Japanese tourists rushed past him. They were obviously late for their flight. One of them looked like they were going to bang into the violin. Kennedy, a master at this, changed his body position so that she bumped into his side instead. She looked at him and gave him a very apologetic look. Kennedy gave a gesture with his hand to show that he was not worried. Had she bumped into the violin, well, it would have been a different story.

"Everything alright?" Beverley asked.

"Yeah, no problem, just a wayward Japanese."

He smiled and checked his Jaeger-Le-Coultre watch. A seriously tasty timepiece, but not flash. A temptation which he had been unable to resist during his lucrative musician days. Murray had picked the watch up duty free at Osaka. He'd been playing with an orchestra which had been booked by the British Council. Some cultural exchange deal with Japan. Nearly bought himself a Rolex, but was glad he hadn't. (Ray's muscle-bound mate had a Rolex as big as a steam-roller.)

"You sound normal, now." Beverley's tone was teasing.

"Sorry." He readjusted the strap as it was cutting into his shoulder.

"A second ago you sounded like you were in the mood for some action." She laughed.

"A second ago I was. In fact I still am." He breathed heavily down the phone.

"What are you wearing? Why don't you moan down the phone at me," he said suggestively.

"Are you ready for this?" She whispered in a deep and sexy voice.

"Yes. But you better be quick. A 747 waits for no man."

"I'm wearing rubber gloves and I haven't stopped. Been at it all morning, washing scrubbing, dishwasher you name it and I was giving Milly a bath when you rang."

"What?" Kennedy was taken aback.

"Well, you did say to tell you what I was wearing and to moan down the phone. There you go. " She was laughing out loud.

"Yeah right." He felt his trousers go limp. Served him right.

"Just quickly before I go. How's Milly?" His flight was about to close. He was very near to the gate, but he would have to get a move on.

"Still thinks she's nobody."

"Shit!" He meant that twice over as his money ran out.

He left the receiver dangling as he ran for the gate. If he'd looked over his shoulder and down at the cars below, he would have seen the parked Citroen and Raoul sitting at the wheel playing with his waxed moustache. But as far as Kennedy knew, Raoul was long gone and in the centre of Paris by now.

Kennedy settled into his business class seat on the Air France 747. He always flew business class when he could. The oxygen seemed better up front and the steak and wine were an additional plus. Before he knew it they were in the air and he had struck up a conversation with a very pleasant flight attendant who usually split her time between London and New York. Her name was Patricia, and Kennedy felt his mouth go a little bit dry as she reminded him of Beverley. She had to tend to the needs of the other passengers, so after a while Kennedy nodded off.

The plane landed safely at J.F.K. Through the high glass panels of the arrivals lounge he could see the weather was turning nasty. He headed for customs, the violin tucked under one arm and his case under the other. He had no problem going through. Maxim always saw to it that if there was anything he could do to smooth the passage of a piece and the courier responsible for it, then it was done.

Kennedy waited at customs whilst the violin was inspected manually. No-one let out a gasp like he had when they opened up the case. Obviously they weren't music lovers. He thanked the female inspector, she smiled.

10

The clouds had gathered and the first lashings of rain began to fall. Kennedy was surprised to find that there was no-one to greet him. He waited for a while trying to see if any of the signs being held up included his name, but they didn't. He was irritated, it was unusual to be kept waiting. Whenever he went on one of Maxim's jobs there was always a driver there for him. He turned full circle, the violin tucked tightly against his body, but still there was no-one around for him. He sighed and leaned against the rail. What to do now? He wasn't sure apart from phoning Maxim. He'd now been in the arrivals lounge for about twenty minutes. Any further deliberation was cut short by a voice in his ear.

"Mister Kennedy?"

Kennedy turned to see who was speaking. Indistinct looking, he was of medium height, with a raincoat and neat scarf tied around his neck. A small enamel badge carried the logo of the New York City Symphony Orchestra.

"I'm sorry I'm late, have you been waiting long?" he asked, reaching for Kennedy's case.

"Yeah, well, sort of. Where were you?"

Raincoat sniffed an apology, "The motorway was really busy. Terrible delays, nothing I could do about it." Kennedy couldn't quite place the man's accent.

Raincoat shrugged his shoulders as he started to walk out of the terminal building. Kennedy followed him, noticing that the raincoat didn't really fit him all that well.

"What's your name?" Kennedy shouted above the roar

of jet engines.

"Al, just call me Al." Raincoat didn't look behind him as he spoke. He turned down the approach road leading to the terminal building. There was a sign indicating that the car park was to the right.

"The car park's that way." Kennedy nodded in the opposite direction.

Raincoat Al turned and hesitated, licking his lips. "Yeah right, that was full. There's an overspill this way." He kept walking, hardly glancing over his shoulder. Rain lashed down, a major storm was brewing.

Kennedy was familiar with the layout of the airport. Very familiar. There was no overspill. He called after Raincoat who slowly stopped and turned round. There was something very wrong here.

"Yeah?" Raincoat suddenly didn't look very friendly.

"I'm not going another inch!" Kennedy shouted through the driving rain. He instinctively held the violin closer to his body.

"Is that right. What's up?"

Raincoat slowly walked towards him. Kennedy was about to turn and run but was suddenly glued to the spot.

Two seven inch blades framed both sides of his head, the points just resting inside each ear. He could feel the cold tensile steel against his skin. Kennedy's balls shrunk and his buttocks involuntarily clenched. The blades were held by two thin hands, the owner of which was standing directly behind him. From the very corner of his eye, he noticed a small, unusual looking tattoo just where the thumb and forefinger met; a bird of some sort.

His thoughts were brought back to the present by Raincoat, who was standing directly in front of him. It did not take a rocket scientist to work out that the real driver from the orchestra was lying in a ditch somewhere with a massive headache, or worse.

"I think you know what we want."

Kennedy knew only too well. Raincoat reached forward and Kennedy let his grip on the violin loosen. Raincoat bent forward to take the violin, then stopped.

"You seemed to realise that something was up. What was it?" He was curious.

Kennedy sighed and shot him a steely look which made him appear much braver than he felt. Hatred was welling up in him and was clouding his judgement.

"The man who was supposed to meet me is American. You're not a Yank."

Raincoat smiled. "Very good. How did you know?" Water was dripping off his face and running down the front of his cream shirt.

"Motorway." Kennedy's head was perfectly still. It was almost as if the two hands were disembodied entities suspended in mid-air.

"Motorway?" Raincoat was still in the same position, half bending. The man behind Kennedy wasn't moving a muscle.

"Americans say highway or expressway."

This was beginning to feel like a linguistics lesson. Kennedy was thinking fast. As Raincoat Al started to straighten up, Kennedy felt the pressure of the two knife tips start to bite. A few yards away a car pulled up. Kennedy could just make out the late model Buick and it's two passengers. They didn't move, but their heads were turned in his direction. Obviously transport for the violin. He had a choice. Do something or die. He breathed in through his nose, his stomach inflating but his chest remaining perfectly still. In one smooth, hard, strike he swiftly brought his right hand up to the underside of captor's right hand and forced the blade out of his ear and away from his head. He shifted his weight onto his right leg and as he did so he felt the point of the knife in his left ear start to penetrate.

Kennedy twisted his neck with savage ferocity, forcing the thrust of the knife past his face and into a soft fleshy mass— Raincoat. The long slim blade was buried handle deep, into his throat. He made no noise as he died. Pai-Lan stepped forward catching Raincoat's body in his right arm, making sure the violin wouldn't be slammed onto the ground. He allowed the dead man to slip slowly to the concrete, cushioning the violin as he went. He shouted in Chinese for the two men in the car (one of whom was already half out of the passenger seat) to take custody of the Amati.

Pai-Lan's other knife was now back in his grip. He looked in the direction that Kennedy had run and broke into a run behind him. There was blood flowing out of Kennedy's ear and a trail of snot coming out of his nose as he ran for his life. Suddenly he lost his footing and fell to the ground. The noise of his elbow cracking could be heard even above the sound of plane engines and the wind whirling around him. One thing was for sure, death awaited him if he stayed on the ground. He kept rolling and allowed his momentum to carry him back to his feet. He regained his balance and turned towards the restricted area where the baggage handlers clocked in. He knew that the distraction of lights and noise in that section represented his only chance of survival. His heart was pumping in his chest so hard he thought it would jump out. Two baggage handlers stood open mouthed as he crashed into view, his trousers ripped and his leg gashed from his fall. He stopped and fell to one knee. The two baggage handlers looked at him. With his injured right arm, he tried to point toward his assailants, but the two could see nothing. Pai-Lan had wisely retreated into the shadows.

The two handlers, nicknamed Laurel and Hardy because one was short and fat and the other tall and thin, stood in horror. Laurel was the first to catch Kennedy before he fell to the ground. Kennedy knew he was going to be sick so they helped him into the toilet. Laurel stayed in the toilet whilst Hardy called the police. The right thing to do under the circumstances.

Kennedy sat on the closed toilet seat inside the cubicle and was sick on the floor. He didn't have the energy to lift the toilet lid and then when he had finished throwing up he started to cry. The tears were thick and came from deep inside. It was the first time he had cried since Debbie had died. The violin was like losing a part of him. Another thing ripped from him without permission and he had been powerless to do anything about it. He was sick again as he continued to cry.

11

He was still weeping when Hardy came in with Senior Officer O'Rourke of New York's fifth precinct. Tears may warm the hearts of most ordinary men but O'Rourke was no ordinary man. Some of his juniors even suggested that he was heartless, but never dared say it within earshot. That was not the swift route to promotion.

O'Rourke hated crying, especially in men. Gone were the days when men could be expected to behave with dignity and stoicism. He couldn't stand it. God knows what his old dad would have made of it, were he still alive. O'Rourke senior's life had been forged in the steel furnaces of New Jersey. A man of few words, no-one had ever known what he was thinking. To O'Rourke's knowledge no living man or woman had ever seen his father cry. In a drunken conversation one night, some cheeky rookie had suggested to O'Rourke that if his father had cried more he would have lived past the age of fifty-nine. A bar stool across the head brought that conversation to a quick close. O'Rourke had been very lucky, the injured party had not pressed charges and there were no witnesses willing to discuss it. Nevertheless, he got a warning from his super and a very nasty slap on the wrist. His step had been watched for quite a while after that.

Now he was a detective in Manhattan's 5th precinct, New York's Chinatown. Tonight he had two headaches. One was professional and had brought him all the way out to the airport, not his normal haunt, in the rain. The other was inside his head and was threatening to burst out of his throbbing temples. He stroked his furrowed brow, twirled his trilby (yes trilby) between his thumb and forefinger and looked over at the hunched figure of Kennedy, still sitting on the can. He shook his umbrella and a few drops of water dripped onto the grimy floor. He allowed himself a few sarcastic thoughts as he got a glimpse of the yellow sign warning of a slippery surface that had just been cleaned. An umbrella was all but useless in this kind of wind and rain. His shirt stuck to him as a few remaining raindrops rolled down his back and gathered around his cheap trouser belt.

The neon light of the toilet reflected off of Officer Caruso's buttons as he came over to where O'Rourke was standing. "The limey's pretty shook up. Better take it easy, Boss." He smiled gently at O'Rourke. O'Rourke's eyebrow lifted. Take it easy was not in his vocabulary. There was a tic in his jaw as he made his way over to where Kennedy was sitting.

"I'm O'Rourke of the fifth precinct." He fixed the Brit with what was supposed to look like a kindly stare, to put him at his ease. What it looked like was an irritated scowl. Kennedy did not look up so O'Rourke started to repeat himself.

"I said, I'm..." He didn't manage to finish his sentence, Kennedy interrupted him.

"I heard you," replied Kennedy looking straight ahead. His tear stained face was tired and drawn and there was still blood leaking out of one of his ears where Pai-Lan's knife had caught him. O'Rourke found his gaze being drawn to it.

"You were lucky." He scratched his face and the muscle tic stopped. He was pleased, it irritated him. It made him look nervous when he wasn't. Disturbed his karma.

"What?"

"I said you were lucky," he repeated.

Kennedy blinked back the moisture in his eyes and

gave O'Rourke a quizzical look.

"Our Chinese friends have been busy the last few days. You weren't supposed to live through this one." He found it difficult to keep the scornful look off his face as he addressed Kennedy.

"Apart from the fact they didn't bother to cover up their faces there's another little thing." O'Rourke didn't bother to try to look too sympathetic.

"What's that?" Kennedy felt like shit. He couldn't get up from the toilet seat even if he'd wanted to.

"The man with the knives, the one you didn't see." O'Rourke played with his teeth at the front as though he had a piece of food lodged there.

"Yeah." Kennedy was quiet, he wasn't sure he wanted to hear what was coming next.

"He treats one of the blades with poison."

O'Rourke continued to pick at his teeth. Another night it would have irritated the hell out of Kennedy but there was enough to concentrate on at the moment.

"Which one?" Kennedy knew what was coming next as soon as he said it. O'Rourke was an obvious smartass, as they say in the States.

"The one that didn't cut you. It seems he likes to play the odds. Only he never seems to lose."

"Do you know who he is?" Kennedy felt the cut in his ear and instinctively touched the other. There was no need, had there been a cut he would have been dead by now.

"Triad. They've got a finger in every pie. This guy takes care of business himself...deadly nightshade," he continued after a short pause.

"Sorry?" Kennedy suddenly felt very tired and the sadness at the loss of the violin was overwhelming. He felt like a loser in everything. All he cared about seemed to slip through his fingers like sand. He even started to think about Milly and Beverley. He took a deep breath and told himself not to even go there.

"Deadly nightshade," he repeated. O'Rourke made it sound like an answer from the quiz show. The one with the phone a friend, ask the audience or go fifty fifty.

"As far as we can make out, your friend dips the tip of his knife in deadly nightshade so even a prick from the blade will kill you."

Kennedy tried to stand up from the seat. O'Rourke did not try to help him as he stood with his back to him, whilst he spoke. The sound of Kennedy crashing back on his bottom told him, the attempt had failed.

"Actually it seems that he only dips the tip of one blade in the poison as a kind of private Russian roulette to see if the one with the poison gets a scratch in." He looked in the mirror. Kennedy was only a grimy reflection. O'Rourke made a mental note to mention the state of the toilets on the way out.

Caruso returned. He had been sorting out some loose ends, seeing if there had been any other witnesses to the night's goings-on apart from Laurel and Hardy. He was sweating slightly, which O'Rourke found a little surprising since it wasn't hot in the airport. In fact, it was a little on the cool side. O'Rourke looked at Caruso who nodded back at him. O'Rourke turned to Kennedy.

"You up to moving yet?" The question may have sounded sympathetic but his tone was anything but. Kennedy managed to get to his feet this time.

"Yes," he grunted.

"Good. There's a lot we still have to talk about. You'll go with Caruso. I'll see you back at the precinct."

Caruso took Kennedy by the arm and guided him out of the toilet into the foyer. O'Rourke caught the swinging door just before it slammed back in his face. He watched Caruso and Kennedy disappear then he sniffed and headed for the information desk. He flashed his warrant card at the pretty young girl who was finishing up a phone call.

"Can I help you, officer?" She straightened her shoulders and made her presence felt. O'Rourke kept his eyes straight ahead, although that was easier said than done, she was seriously pretty. She flashed her eyelashes as she blinked a couple of times.

"Yeah, you can. I want to see the supervisor responsible for the restroom cleaning." He smiled as though he meant it, which he did.

"Why has there been a crime done in there?" She laughed at her own joke. O'Rourke didn't answer but the look on his face made it clear he wasn't in the mood for jokes. The smile froze on her face and she tannoyed the supervisor. As O'Rourke waited, his eyes fell on the candy machine by the wall. It was surrounded by wrappers left by people who had actually been successful in getting something out of it. He licked his lips. He loved candy. No, he worshiped it. He felt his pockets but was out of luck, he only had a couple of bills.

Suddenly Caruso reappeared, with Kennedy slightly behind him, looking very sorry for himself.

"What's up?" O'Rourke asked, saliva gathering in his mouth for the candy which his mind had already told his body was to follow. He needed some change and fast.

"I left my uh, keys and stuff in the washroom."

Caruso looked a bit distracted. O'Rourke figured it had been a bit much seeing the remains of Raincoat Al. Caruso was not the most robust of souls. NYPD had employment opportunities for all sorts. Caruso was living proof of this.

"Whatever. You got some change?" O'Rourke got straight to the point.

Caruso had just spent all his change on the phone call he'd made moments ago. Calls to mobiles were expensive.

"No, 'fraid not."

He looked a bit strange. Another night O'Rourke would probably have noticed but tonight was not like any other night. Chinese boys causing havoc in the precinct and now this musical heist at the airport and all in the middle of what was turning out to be a pretty impressive rain storm.

O'Rourke sighed as Caruso went into the restroom leaving Kennedy there. The limey looked really unhappy. Good. O'Rourke would look forward to giving him a hard time back at the station house. Million dollars worth of stuff being carried by a Brit with what looked like a dodgy hand, he shook his head for probably the twentieth time that night. Irritating habit but he liked it.

Caruso came back holding the keys to the squad car. He nodded another farewell to O'Rourke and he and Kennedy headed for the car for the second time that night. A small almost dwarf like figure appeared out of the corner of O'Rourke's eye. He turned to look at the over-grown schoolboy figure in a dark blue overall. A small hand was extended.

"Hi, I'm Alfonso, the supervisor. You wanted to see me?" Alfonso was smiling. He was always happy to help the police in their important work.

O'Rourke didn't even bother looking at him as he spoke. One eye was fixed on where Caruso had been standing, something was now beginning to bother him about what he'd seen, the other was on the candy machine.

"Got a quarter?"

Alfonso's heart sunk and he hesitated. He too, worshiped the candy machine and quarters were not to be given away lightly. However the look on O'Rourke's face had him ferreting around in his trouser pocket, underneath his overalls, for some of the precious silver coins. He slowly took some out of his pocket and deposited them in O'Rourke's waiting hand. If he was was looking for a thanks he was searching in the wrong place. All he got was O'Rourke's back as he bore down on the candy machine.

12

The storm was raging now. Outgoing flights had been cancelled and the last of the planes which had to come in had all landed. The ones still in the sky had been diverted to Newark and La Guardia. Both were acceptable alternatives as the storm front, though vicious, occupied a very narrow corridor.

Caruso looked up at the elements and tightened his collar. "Bad day for a fat boy," he said more to himself than Kennedy.

"Sorry?" Kennedy shouted to make himself heard above the howling wind.

Caruso looked at him, in a kind of distracted way. He didn't look very happy. "I used to be a an air traffic controller." He looked at his watch then pointed to a set of far-off lights in the sky. It was an airliner making its buffeted and unsteady way to Newark."See that?" Caruso also shouted at the top of his voice. It was the only way to make himself heard.

Kennedy nodded, leaning into the wind to stop himself from falling over.

"It's a 747, fat boy It leaves a wake turbulence like you wouldn't believe." He pointed to the fast disappearing form of the Jumbo.

"Wake turbulence?" Kennedy couldn't believe he was having this conversation. There was so much going through his head. Maxim would be broken hearted and would probably never forgive him. Was there nothing he could hold onto? First Debbie, and now this. Was everything of value and worth going to be ripped from his grasp every time they came near to his soul.

"Yeah, like a vortex at the wings. It leaves a massive wave behind it. Bit like a giant liner's bow wave." Caruso wiped some of the rain water off his face which had gathered in the pits and lines of his youngish but stressed skin.

"You know a lot about it." Kennedy shouted. His ears were hurting both from the attack and from the pounding of the gale.

Caruso looked round at Kennedy. "Like I said, I was an air traffic controller. It's what I used to be before I became a cop." He smiled vacantly. It looked more like a grimace.

"Why did you quit?"

"Got sick of the stress. Moved because I thought there would be more money and less grief as a policeman." He gestured at the uniformed shape behind the wheel of a squad car which had approaching very slowly. The shape made a gesture to show he had understood and drove the car level to where Caruso and Kennedy were standing or rather leaning into the wind. The Jumbo was long gone, already making its bumpy and unsteady approach into Newark, just on the edge of the storm.

"Was there?" Kennedy was almost screaming now as he bent his head and got into the back of the blue and white squad car.

"Was there what?" Caruso's by contrast was a quiet whisper now as he was in the front seat and turned round facing Kennedy. Even so his voice sounded like a cannon going off. Deep and booming.

"Less stress and more money?"

"No," Caruso checked his watch, tapped the driver, and gestured for him to get moving, "...there wasn't." He checked his watch again.

"In a hurry?" Kennedy meant no harm by his question but Caruso's response was defensive.

"Waddayamean?" A flash of anger crossed his face.

"Nothing." Kennedy's voice was almost a whisper as he gestured with his good hand. He never talked with the other, just a self-conscious reaction to the injury.

They drove for a few minutes in total silence then Caruso suddenly held his head and made a funny kind of wheezing noise."Jeez, I think I'm going to be sick, take the next turn-off," he hissed through clenched teeth.

The uniform did a double take. As Caruso grimaced in pain, he cut across two lanes causing a pick- up to brake sharply. He sounded his horn and shook his fist as the uniform checked his mirror and began to slow down.

Caruso pointed out of the window. "Not here. Go on over the hill, you can park up there."

"Why?" Uniform liked asking questions. He fancied being a detective himself one day. Caruso sighed then spoke slowly as though he was talking to someone with half a brain.

"I don't want to throw up in full view of half of New York, that's why." He shook his head in despair at having to explain something so obvious.

Uniform smiled, slightly embarrassed that he hadn't guessed so obvious a reason. He accelerated and the supercharged Pontiac glided effortlessly forward to where the road reached a crest, then he stopped. He squinted through the driving rain. There was a car just visible in the distance. He blinked as Caruso quickly got out, presumably to deposit the prawns he'd eaten at the roadside precinct canteen. Just as well I stuck to the lamb, he thought. It was his last, he would never make detective. The thin shiny blade pierced his throat and exited just below his right ear.

13

Kennedy had kicked the door open and rolled onto the water and petrol streaked road, even before the blade had done it's terrible job. He'd seen the knife and the tattooed hand which held it, only seconds before it was plunged into the throat of the junior officer. He got up, and for the second time that night, ran for his life. He looked over his shoulder and saw Caruso and the man with the knife shouting at each other. The terrible realisation that Caruso was part of it all, hit him like a runaway express train. He was fighting for breath as he ran as fast as he could. The sound of the car starting behind him told him, in no uncertain terms, that he was not going to be chased on foot. He turned to the left, slipping heavily in the mud and gravel. His life depended on him getting up as quickly as possible, so he did. His knee was twisted, he could feel the ligaments rubbing against each other. The car screeched to a halt, in a hail of rain water and mud. The knifeman and Caruso leapt out and sprinted after Kennedy.

His breath was firing out of him like machine gun bullets, Uzi style. His eyes were like a hunted dog's, bloodshot and swollen. Death almost seemed like an attractive proposition as his body threatened to give out completely. Then he saw it. A ridge. Looked like a ditch. If he could just get there, maybe he could escape under the cover of darkness. He fell, then stumbled to the ridge and flung himself over what was really an eighty foot drop to the highway below. His head felt like it was going to burst as his body spun round and round like a rag doll. Horns blared in his head as he prepared to die.

Knifeman and Caruso got to the edge a few moments later. Caruso leaned over to try to see what was left of Kennedy. Mistake. A knife sliced through his gut in a deep upward thrust. Caruso heard a whisper in his ear as he died, "I've started, so I'll finish." Caruso remained silent as blood seeped onto the assassin's tattooed hand. The knifeman's eyes were bitter with disappointment. Two hits tonight, plus Kennedy's death plunge and yet none of them had made a sound. Back to the drawing board. Somewhere out there, waiting for him, was someone who would not die in silence.

The crumpled form of Caruso was left where it lay. He was no longer useful now that they had gotten the violin. And Kennedy? Kennedy was a loose end they would have had to sort out anyway...eventually. In the end, things had worked out. He walked slowly back to the car, its blazing lights guided him back through the night. The radio was on and slow blues tunes were blaring from inside the vehicle. The knifeman sat in the driving seat and allowed himself a final thought about Caruso. He'd come to them looking for extra money for less work. Well now he was in a place where he didn't have to worry about money or work Pai-Lan laughed to himself as he ignited the engine. He liked that thought. It pleased him and made him feel good despite the fact none of his victims had squealed for his pleasure. He put the car into drive and slowly rejoined the traffic flow.

A car in an obvious hurry was coming up fast behind him. Pai-Lan pulled into the next lane to let him pass. Ironically, he was a safe and courteous driver. Besides, he didn't have far to go to rejoin his assistant, parked a couple of miles up the freeway. He had waited patiently for Pai-Lan, confident that his superior would have tidied up the loose ends by now. The Amati violin lay safely on the back seat. Little Dragon would be pleased.

14

It was a very bad start to the day for O'Rourke. It had taken him far longer than usual to get to the precinct in Manhattan. His breakfast of waffles and fried eggs, cooked for him by Rosa who came every morning to cook then clean, had not agreed with him. Too much candy the night before. The mess waiting for him downtown did not help his digestion much either. Caruso was dead. O'Rourke was deeply upset. Not about Caruso's untimely end, but about his inability to peg him as a rotten badge. His reputation for picking out the bad cops was renowned throughout New York and he had prided himself on being able to smell a stink. He would never live this down. He'd known Caruso like the back of his hand or so he had thought. And to top things off, the traffic from hell was keeping him gridlocked only a few blocks from the precinct.

He'd had enough. He got onto the two way radio. In typical manner, he did not waste time on the social stuff. "Is Blinker there?" That was his nickname for the latest recruit Eddie Lee, half Chinese half American. Eager to please, O'Rourke was going to enjoy using him as much as possible. Two years ago, Lee had joined the precinct from the Academy. That was considered "fresh" in the fifth precinct. His fluency in several different dialects of Northern Chinese was considered to be of great value by the bosses that be. At the precinct, everyone had laughed because they knew that all the Chinese gangsters spoke perfect English. Well, almost perfect.

"Yes sir, he's here."

The clear resonant voice belonged to Officer Wallace, a young black woman who had been at the station house for several years now. Organised, professional, she took no shit from O'Rourke, and he knew it. Any infantile racist, sexist or generally unwelcome nicknames would have seen him stuck with a harassment suit quicker than he could have said "What's your problem?"

"Good." O'Rourke shouted even though the traffic was at a fairly quiet standstill apart from a few horns and blasphemy being exchanged. "Send him down to me, pronto. I'm just a few blocks away opposite Franco's deli. The traffic ain't moving. Blinker can bring the car in for me and I'll walk."

He adjusted his position in the car. Damn leather seats. Even in the winter they made him sweat, stuck to his backside and creased his trousers.

"Very good, sir. I'll tell him right away," Wallace's voice came back clear, sharp, and correct.

"How's it all looking?" O'Rourke did a double-take at Franco's deli. It looked tempting but then the rumble in his belly reminded him of it's delicate state. He groaned.

"Sorry, sir?" Wallace heard something but wasn't sure what it was.

"Nothing." O'Rourke snapped. He was embarrassed that his stomach could have been heard over a short wave radio. Technology, it just gets fancier and fancier every day. "I said how's it looking?"

"Pretty bad, sir. A lot of mess to sort out. All waiting for you." She said the last part with slightly more enthusiasm than O'Rourke appreciated and she knew it but she was still correct and clear so he had to take it on the chin. The traffic was still at a complete standstill. O'Rourke could have used his light and siren but there was nowhere for anyone to go.

"Morning, sir." Lee was polite and saluted, an appropriate but unusual sign of reverence for a police officer, it made O'Rourke slightly uncomfortable.

O'Rourke got out of the car, leaving the keys in the ignition and the motor running. He licked his lips as he looked at the deli. His stomach was feeling considerably better, but now there wasn't any time for a snack. Lee smiled and slid into the still warm seat which had been vacated by O'Rourke.

"Take it to the precinct house?" Lee looked up at O'Rourke who was lost in thought.

"Hmm, what?" He looked down at Lee sitting in the driver's seat and realised that he had come within a whisper of calling him Blinker. This would have been a bit much and O'Rourke knew that even the placid Lee may well have been stung into some kind of work place grievance if he'd been subjected to such humiliation. Then he looked again at the grinning, blinking uniformed officer and he wasn't so sure.

"Take it back to the precinct, sir?" Lee was good manners personified and there wasn't a hint of impatience in his voice. Wasn't his way. In truth, he was not stupid at all, and was aware of a lot more than many, including his superiors, actually realised.

"Yup. See you back there." O'Rourke nodded and closed the door, trapping part of Lee's slightly oversized police jacket in the door. He opened it again, allowing Lee to pull it in.

"Sorry Lee, didn't see it." O'Rourke acknowledged.

"No problem, sir."

He smiled up at O'Rourke again, waited a bit, then said "Sir?"

"What?" O'Rourke answered a bit impatiently. Lee, still smiling, nodded at the driver's door which was still open and being leaned on by O'Rourke; Lee wasn't going anywhere. O'Rourke made an apologetic gesture and stepped back closing the door with slightly more force than was necessary. He sighed, turned and started walking to the precinct station. He was lost in thought as he walked slowly along the street. Last night's rain water splashed onto his brightly polished shoes.

He stopped in front of a sparkling clean shop window, and examined his face. Big. Beginnings of a second chin. His father had been jowly so it followed that he would be, eventually. Some sessions in the sauna or a few more squash games would probably have done the trick but he hated all that heaving and sweating. Always made him feel like he was one step away from a heart attack. A good glass of Bourbon and a smoke of one of his favourite cigars, round the corner from the precinct in Cactus Jack's, was his idea of fun. Mind you there was no getting away from the fact his face, belly and butt were packing more flesh than was necessary.

With a deep breath, he looked through the window at an impressive display of expensive designer clothes. They would have to sew two outfits together to fit a frame his size and even then the seams would be working overtime. And the price tags were unbelievable! No ordinary policeman would have been able to afford them.

Was this what was at the root of Caruso's defection? Did he sell out to the Chinese gangsters so that he could afford a lifestyle his policeman's wage couldn't buy him? O'Rourke looked puzzled as he thought to himself. Shitty clothes which fell apart in a bit of rain and flashy watches which never told the time properly anyway. Was that it? Buying some expensive yacht and cruising to ports inhabited by people who still didn't want to know you if you were wearing the wrong tie. These damn boats cost a million dollars a metre and the smallest ones were seventy metres long. Lottery winners couldn't afford them. The purchase of some empty tin dream. He felt incredibly angry with Caruso, he'd believed he could have gone a long way in the force.

O'Rourke was a contradiction, and rubbed many

people the wrong way. He was racist, homophobic, and regarded women with disdain. (Just as well he'd never married.) O'Rourke was many things which people found hard to take but he was straight. He was a clean cop and he couldn't be bought. Many had tried over the years as he'd worked his way up through the force but none had been successful. Gangsters would try to buy him and then they would try to scare him with their threats. They always succeeded in scaring him. O'Rourke was too clever not to take threats seriously, particularly when they came from the Chinese. And by taking the threats to heart, he showed respect to a people who would die before losing face. That was the main reason O'Rourke had a high level of success in policing Chinatown, he understood the concept of face. He took them seriously but he hated them all, even the good ones. His racism ran deep.

He pulled himself together and his thoughts snapped back to the present. There was something heavy going on in Chinatown. The snatching of the violin was big bucks made easy, although he wasn't too sure about who would fence such an unusual item. Probably end up behind the electrified door of some mentally ill gangster who had a penchant for playing the violin but couldn't on account his thumbs had been broken far too often. The theft of the musical instrument was one thing but there was something else that recently had happened in Chinatown. Ka-Lut, daughter of Wo-Kei, one of the most influential and powerful triad leaders operating out of Vancouver, had been kidnapped. She had come to New York to start her musical studies at the prestigious School of Music. This was going to start some kind of war unless it had already started. He was sure there was a link between the violin and the girl from Vancouver.

Unfortunately, the goings-on at the airport had happened just in time to catch late press. He mumbled a greeting to Louie who had been selling papers there ever since O'Rourke could remember. Some cash changed hands and O'Rourke groaned as he looked at the headlines. Two dead, world famous violin stolen. Chaos at JFK. The sad truth was that no-one had actually noticed what had happened at the airport apart from the baggage handlers, and the people directly involved in the theft. O'Rourke walked, paper in hand, into the entrance of the precinct. What he saw next, half sprawled across the reception bench, was what looked like a dead man leaning.

15

Kennedy had looked better, but he was alive, that was what mattered the most. Fate had dealt him a kind blow. He owed his life to a scaffolder's cradle suspended a few feet under the ledge he'd gone over. The wind had pushed it out just far enough to catch him when he fell and the same wind had blown it back so that Pai-Lan had not seen him when he'd looked over the parapet. He'd spent the night in the hospital so he could be examined. His ear was in the most pain, aside from his heart.

An armed police guard had been assigned to his room though he doubted that anyone would come looking for a dead man. Kennedy had resisted police efforts for him to use his "death" to further the case. He'd agreed to speak with O'Rourke, but after that he planned to be on the next plane back to Britain, away from all of this madness.

Kennedy stood up when O'Rourke gestured with his head to the door he was holding open. He walked through it. O'Rourke shouted at the desk sergeant, a grizzly bear in human form who went by the name of Lawrence. No-one knew if that was his first or last name. He'd never volunteered the information so no-one ever asked. Even the most dramatic of criminals stopped acting large when they clapped eyes on Lawrence. He had no neck, his head connected straight to his body and his eyes looked like drill holes in a dead piece of wood. If he hadn't been in uniform you would have thought he had just shaken off his straight jacket. In some ways the uniform made him look worse. People joked that he'd been the inspiration for the low budget movie "Lunatic Cop." There was probably more to that than people realised since the director of that film lived only a few blocks away and he was always in on parking ticket violations or arranging for filming passes with the traffic division.

"When Blin..I mean Lee gets here, send him straight in, I want him to sit in on the interview with the ..."

"Limey." Kennedy finished the sentence for O'Rourke.

"Yeah, whatever."

The grunt which came back from the sergeant told him that his request had registered. It looked like Lawrence was smiling but then O'Rourke realised that he was just having a silent sniff. Head cold, the poor weather didn't agree with him. He would be glad when the summer came and he and his elderly mother could get some well needed rays of warmth in their bones.

O'Rourke closed the door behind him and went over to the coffee machine sitting by the side. He pointed a cup at Kennedy who shook his head.

"You want something else?" he asked as he poured himself a cup of the hot wet stuff. A couple of creamers and too much sugar finished off the concoction.

"I doubt you'd have it."

Kennedy's accent got on O'Rourke's nerves and as the American had a glass face, it showed. O'Rourke gave Kennedy a look which could have frozen the Hudson.

"Buddy, this is America, we have everything. You name it, we got it." He took a sip of his steaming hot coffee.

Kennedy gave O'Rourke a similar look back, but after his previous night's experience, it lacked the necessary power to fuel the venom, he undoubtedly felt. You asked for it, he thought to himself as the door opened and they were joined by a smiling Lee.

"Kennedy, this is Officer Lee, he will be sitting in while I conduct my interview." Lee nodded at Kennedy and sat down at the far end of the room.

"I'd like some meadowsweet, please," Kennedy said on

second thought. He looked directly at O'Rourke who held his gaze without looking away. They would probably have stayed like that for all eternity if Lee hadn't interjected.

"It's an herbal tea." He seemed quite pleased with himself and blinked for good measure.

O'Rourke did not turn to look at Lee, as he spoke. "Is that right?"

He almost sounded Texan in the way he slowed his words right down for this one. Lee nodded, then realised the futility of that action when he realised that O'Rourke wasn't actually looking at him. He had his eyes fixed firmly on the Brit. Kennedy, uncomfortable as a result of his injuries, shifted in his seat. He hated that it seemed as though he was reacting to O'Rourke's gaze.

"It's antacid, very effective," he said trying to speak slowly like O'Rourke. Instead of sounding Texan, Kennedy just managed to sound like he came from Wales.

"Is that so?" O'Rourke said very dryly, but a little quicker this time.

"Of course, if you don't have that I would be happy with black horehound," he said hopefully.

"That sounds like someone from the titty bars on Broadway," O'Rourke said without humour.

Lee joined in again. He really was an awful judge of when to speak and when to stay quiet. "Black horehound, it works well against nausea."

"Or failing that, I would be happy with some ginger." Kennedy looked O'Rourke straight in the eye and this time managed not to look away. Not an easy task, under the circumstances.

"Ginger, I've got some of that." Lee stood up with an excited look on his face. "I'll get it for you."

He headed for the door without checking with O'Rourke. This did not please him, he should have asked.

"Lee." O'Rourke said quietly.

Stilted and awkward, Lee came to an instant standstill by the door. "Yes sir?" He blinked again and swallowed.

"Isn't there something else?"

O'Rourke was waiting for Lee to ask for permission to go for the tea. Lee stood there for a moment then something seemed to dawn on him.

"Oh, yes. Ginger. It is really good if your stomach is a bit upset. Settles it very well." He smiled, pleased with himself that he and Kennedy were educating O'Rourke in the ways of herbs and their associated properties.

O'Rourke swayed his head from side to side and licked his lips.

"Lee," he sniffed.

"Yes sir?" Lee had his hand on the handle of the door leading back out to the entrance hall of the precinct house.

"Get the tea, now." The word "now" was pronounced with such an edge that it seemed to help propel the young officer out of the room. O'Rourke looked back at Kennedy who continued to stare straight back.

"Do you drink a lot of alcohol?" he asked, although the shade of O'Rourke's skin—a florid red—told the answer.

"I like a drink, yes." O'Rourke admitted.

"Angelica's good for you then." Kennedy smiled without any warmth.

"Who's she?"

"Not a she, a—"

"Don't tell me. A tea," O'Rourke spat.

"How did you guess?" Kennedy said dryly.

"Naturally clever, I guess."

"Angelica results in a distaste for alcohol, if you consume it before you actually start drinking."

"Why should I want to do that?"

"Because it's not good for you," Kennedy said rather smugly.

O'Rourke looked him up and down. "And you're the

example of looking good are you?" he said.

"Someone tried to kill me—twice, and I landed into a metal swing at a rate of knots. Hardly conducive to looking your best, wouldn't you agree Detective?" He made the word "detective", sound like an insult. He meant to. The discussion was cut short when Lee reappeared, with a steaming hot cup of ginger tea.

He gave it to Kennedy who took it gratefully. He couldn't help recognising the ornate dragons on the side of the delicate china cup which held the brew. Lee saw him clock them.

"The tea tastes better from the proper cup. I had it in my locker." He smiled. Lee was obviously a reasonable and gentle man.

"Alright," snapped O'Rourke who was obviously neither nor gentle.

"...enough herb talk. Let's get down to business, Lee." He gestured for him to sit down, as he placed himself opposite Kennedy.

"Aren't you going to turn on a tape recorder or something?" Kennedy asked, genuinely interested. O'Rourke squinted at him; he was beginning to get used to his range of strange looks. The American had quite a lot of them in his repertoire.

"It isn't that kind of interview, unless you've got something to hide of course," he said. The sound of the traffic outside told him that it was all on the move again. Horns, obscenities being shouted in every conceivable language, the clang of bins being emptied, sirens wailing. He loved this city, but the verdict was out on the actual people who inhabited it.

"The only thing I had to hide has already gone," Kennedy said sadly. Lee smiled. It was completely inappropriate, as it wasn't meant to be funny. O'Rourke looked puzzled for a moment, then it dawned on him—the violin.

"You have a funny way of hiding things, especially something so valuable."

"It's the way it's done. Instruments like that are carried all over the world by people like me, it's the safest way." He drank some of the hot ginger tea. Very good.

"Doesn't look very safe to me. You got pretty roughed up last night. We both know you're very lucky to be alive after all that." For the first time since they met, he actually looked concerned. Must have been a trick of the morning light.

"Have you ever been to India?" Kennedy asked. This threw O'Rourke somewhat.

"Why do you ask?"

"Well, gems are transported all over that continent, mainly diamonds. Millions, probably billions of dollars worth every year. How do you think they are moved from one place to another?"

Kennedy enjoyed his shift from questionee to questioner. O'Rourke thought for a moment.

"I dunno, Fedex, UPS. Some kind of secure force." He offered a range of likely alternatives. The noise coming in from the street outside was now almost deafening. Neither Lee or O'Rourke noticed it. This was New York, more particularly Chinatown. Manhattan's fifth precinct, a seething, living mass of Oriental cultures and subcultures which would take a lifetime to describe, identify, or completely understand.

"No. You're wrong on all counts," Kennedy said a little too smugly for O'Rourke's liking. He did not like being wrong about anything. It was his natural competitive spirit as well as a dislike for most things human. Even he knew he had to watch his complete disdain for the human race. He put it down to being a cop for too long and being exposed to the underbelly of humanity. So much exposure that he may have forgotten that not everyone was bad. He would, however take some convincing on that subject.

Kennedy took another sip of his tea and smiled, more for effect than because the tea was nice. He also adjusted his aching body into a more comfortable position. That was not for effect, it really did hurt. He felt like he'd been stood on by an elephant.

Kennedy continued, "About ninety per cent of the gems transported in the Indian subcontinent are carried by couriers who all work for one family firm. They are completely trustworthy and look like everyone else who travels third class on the railway or by bus. They keep the gems in dirty old sacks or satchels, and by their side all the time. Losses are very rare. Usually a forgetful courier who leaves the train without his bag. Doesn't happen very often as you can imagine.

"Why like that?" O'Rourke was interested, though he tried not to appear it.

"It's safer. The big secure outfits are being targeted all the time for robberies and heists. He finished the last of his tea and looked at the remains in the bottom of his cup. If he was looking to the dregs for guidance or inspiration he was to be disappointed. He put it carefully back on the table, aware that it was Lee's personal property.

"The only way that things are stolen is when there is a tip-off. Someone knows what they are looking for and whom." Kennedy felt a dark look cross his battered features. He suddenly felt very tired.

"As far as your violin is concerned, there's nothing surprising in that. The Five Circle boys know everything. Nothing happens that they don't know something about." O'Rourke resembled a kind of worldly scholar as he stood there imparting his knowledge about things criminal. All that was needed was a tweed suit, a pair of broken glasses and some sunlight streaming through the window in that ivy league sort of way.

"Five Circles?" Kennedy asked.

"Triad. Very Chinese, very big, very powerful and very,

very dangerous."

"Who are they?"

"That's the whole point. It's really difficult to pinpoint members or to accurately guess the size of their organisation." O'Rourke drained the last of his coffee and went over and poured some more.

"The man last night, who tried to kill me—he had a little bird tattooed on his hands. Blue, looked like a swallow," Kennedy said. He was trying to be helpful.

"Pai-Lan. They don't come any dirtier. He's always one step ahead. You're a lucky man. They don't usually get away from that one." O'Rourke said. The drama in his voice was not really necessary. Kennedy was paying attention.

"One thing's for sure," he continued with just a glance at Lee who was completely engrossed, "the Five Circle boys have been very busy recently. There's a lot going on, some of it may be connected, then again maybe not."

"How do you mean?"

"A couple a days ago, a young girl was kidnapped. No sign of her so far. No ransom demand, no note, no nothing. She got lifted at JFK. She was coming in from Vancouver to start her musical studies."

"Yes." Kennedy listened intently although it wasn't easy above the roar of traffic and everything else.

"She was easy pickings. She was travelling alone and they sent one of their guys to meet her at the airport."

"And?" Kennedy was like a small child hurrying along a parent who was taking too long to get to the meaty part of a story.

"Not been seen since. The thing was, she should have been completely safe."

"Why?"

"She's the daughter of Wo-Kei. The boss of the Vancouver, Five Circle Boys. She should not have been touched here in New York. Something's going on between the Manhattan triad and the Vancouver one."

"Like what?" There was a knock at the door. O'Rourke nodded at Lee who stood up and opened it. Another uniformed officer walked in.

"Excuse me, sir. We've got the Frenchman on the phone for you." O'Rourke followed him without a word and was gone for several minutes. Kennedy felt his heart sink. He'd been dreading this moment. O'Rourke returned and motioned to Kennedy.

"Your turn."

Kennedy followed him out of the door and he went into the telephone booth which O'Rourke pointed out. It was not an easy call. There was a kind of strangled gasp at the end of the phone, it was Maxim.

"I am so sorry, Maxim."

He could hear a stifled moan then the familiar voice on the end of the line.

"How could this have happened?" Then his thoughts came out in one jumble. "I am ruined, no-one will ever use me again. Such a beautiful thing, the most perfect instrument I have ever seen in my life. Gone, destroyed for all we know. I don't know what to say." His voice trailed off into the distance.

"It all happened so quickly, Maxim. There wasn't time to think."

"I am so upset. I can't talk now, Goodbye."

The conversation was brought swiftly to an end. Kennedy was left looking at the end of the now dead phone line. He looked at Officer Lawrence and motioned that the call was over. Lawrence flicked some switches and the line was transferred back to the front desk. Kennedy went back into the interview room. O'Rourke was pouring himself some more coffee.

"How was it?" He asked as he sat down.

"How do you think?" Kennedy asked. Suddenly he was so tired. All he wanted was to sleep, anywhere, it didn't have to be a bed.

"You were saying about the stuff between the Vancouver and New York boys." Kennedy brought O'Rourke back to the original topic of discussion.

"Yeah." He looked at Lee before continuing. If he didn't blink he was smiling. He was always doing one or the other. "There's a terrible scene of smuggling people into New York from China. They pay what they can for passage, and work off the rest in the hopes that they can start a new life here. But they can never earn enough to pay their debt to the triad. The cost they're charged is just too high."

"Where does Vancouver come in?" Kennedy was beginning to feel a little less tired.

"They bring them in on the coast of British Columbia. It is so massive it's impossible to police properly and once they're in Vancouver they don't stand out because there is such a large Chinese community living there." He poured himself yet another cup of coffee. Both Lee and Kennedy looked at him disapprovingly. His level of caffeine intake was seriously over the top.

"What?" he said defensively.

"The amount of coffee you drink. It's not good for you," Kennedy said.

"And you're the expert, are you?" O'Rourke held his cup closer to him as though he was likely to be the victim of a snatch squad.

"I like coffee, it's just I know that certain types of tea are better for you, that's all."

O'Rourke didn't answer.

"You were saying?" Kennedy realised he was not going to get anywhere advising this man about his health.

"Once they're in Vancouver they are smuggled across land, through the old Indian reservations which are equally impossible to keep an eye on because of their size and sensitive nature. As you can imagine, we just can't roam around them in four wheel drives." He put his coffee cup back on the table. The coffee machine blew a steamy raspberry, almost in defiance to the other two men, in the interview room.

"They come from South East China in specially converted grain boats. They hold anything between two to four hundred people. Each boat turns a profit of around nine million dollars. So you can see the stakes are high. Once these poor idiots get to New York, they're little better than slaves. The Vancouver triad get them here and the New York ones keep them in place."

"Don't people back home get wise to it all?" Kennedy asked not unreasonably.

O'Rourke shrugged his shoulders. "Any rumours are disregarded. People who dream of getting to the Golden Mountain are not interested in bad stories coming back from people already there. They just think they're greedy and don't want anyone else to join in the new life. That's people for you." He raised his eyebrows and looked back at the coffee machine and pursed his lips.

"Golden Mountain?" Kennedy asked.

This time it was Lee who spoke. "My people call New York the Golden Mountain because it is the land of bulging wallets and golden dreams. It's true about others not listening to what they hear. They are desperate. The economic collapse in Asia has not helped things. There are even more people who think the answer is to come to the West. The gangsters are just parasites feeding off peoples' dreams and their hopes for themselves and their kids." This time he was not smiling as he spoke.

O'Rourke definitely needed another cup of coffee. He'd never heard Lee speak so much in one sentence. He didn't hesitate, he headed straight for it but found it empty. "We'll take a break and I'll get some more water for this." He looked like a naughty schoolboy as he went out the door with the jug in his hand.

Kennedy looked out at the entrance area; a little man was standing at the desk, raising his voice at Officer Lawrence. Not a very good idea. The man began to realise that and sat down by the desk, holding a scuffed leather briefcase precisely on his knee. O'Rourke looked over his shoulder at Lawrence who nodded his head to let him know that he would deal with it. O'Rourke came back in and closed the door behind him.

"Wo-Kei is seriously pissed about his daughter. Twenty years old, pretty as a picture, living the American dream and she gets snatched by people who he's supposed to be doing business with." O'Rourke switched the coffee machine on and briefly stepped back to watch his handiwork. He sat down again and faced Kennedy, although one eye was on the coffee machine.

"Ka-Lut is the most important thing in Wo-Kei's life. It seems there must be a dispute over all this and she is the best bargaining power the New York boys could get their hands on."

Lee added, "The word is that Wo-Kei is beside himself with rage but there is also a feeling that if she isn't returned unharmed it would break him like a china cup. Which might be what they want. It's all a bit strange. This is not very Chinese, you know. They usually work things out."

"Even the gangsters?" Kennedy was surprised.

"Especially the gangsters, they see themselves as business men trying to turn a profit. This kind of stuff, kidnapping and the like is seen as low class."

"And the violin?" Kennedy asked.

"That's strange too. Alright it's worth a million but to whom? None of it adds up." The funny little noise from the machine told O'Rourke that the coffee was ready. O'Rourke gave Lee a nod which made it clear he wanted him to leave. O'Rourke suspected that Kennedy was as clean as a whistle and not hiding anything, but he had to be sure.

Once Lee was out of the room, O'Rourke turned to Kennedy.

"What happened to your hand?"

So Kennedy told him the whole story from start to finish. About the accident, his career, his kid, his lover, everything. At the end he was crying again. O'Rourke hated that. Emotion always made him feel uncomfortable. Brits!

His tears were still wet on his face, when Lee came back into the room.

"Mister Kennedy, there's a gentleman waiting to see you from the New York City Symphony Orchestra.

Gentleman was a generous description. Mr Laffe certainly looked like a man of decency and honour, but his colourful language and complete disregard for Kennedy's close call with death was not the stuff normally associated with gentile individuals. Kennedy got the full brunt of his anger and wrath at the theft of the violin. The man from the symphony orchestra was not amused and it was clear that he held Kennedy directly responsible. Kennedy took what was flung at him, as New York's choicest crims and people down on their luck criss-crossed between, in front and behind them. He listened, but he couldn't take his eyes off the scruffy unpolished shoes on Laffe's feet. Mr Laffe seemed disappointed that Kennedy would be staying overnight at the Waldorf, as originally planned. The look on his face as he stormed out made it clear that he would have been happier if it had been a filthy old seaman's mission down by the docks, complete with damp mattress and over- friendly cockroaches.

"God, he was angry," Kennedy said as much to himself as to Lee, who was standing some way off. The truth was that Kennedy knew exactly how Laffe felt. He, too, was finding it extremely difficult to come to terms with all that had happened.

"Looks like our friend could have done with some herbal tea," Lee said smiling and blinking.

O'Rourke came over to where Kennedy was standing with Lee. A large unhappy looking prostitute was being booked at the desk, screaming at everyone, asking them "who did they think she was, a prostitute?" Lawrence was dealing with her. He was doing well. Officer Lawrence dealt expertly with everyone regardless of their social standing or chosen career path, legal or otherwise.

"You're staying at the hotel which was booked for you tonight?" O'Rourke asked, although he already knew the answer. Kennedy nodded. His head hurt like hell, but not as much as his heart.

"Lee will drive you there—if he can find the way." The last part of the sentence was said with a heavy trace of unpleasant sarcasm which did not seem to register with Lee, who still stood there smiling and blinking.

"You were pretty rude to him." Kennedy was nothing if not blunt.

O'Rourke looked at the disappearing form of the little Chinese American."You mean Blinker?" He laughed.

"I don't think that's very funny," Kennedy said. O'Rourke kept his gaze on where Lee had gone then turned to look at O'Rourke.

"I don't care a fat fanny about what you think." His eyes were not friendly, not at all. Kennedy had to think for a moment before he realised that the word "fanny" had a different meaning here in America.

"Alright he may be straight, which is more than can be said for Caruso, but he's not much use for anything except ferrying people around," O'Rourke said.

"Limeys," Kennedy said with a deadpan expression.
"What?"
"You were going to say Limeys, not people. Just say what you mean."

Kennedy and O'Rourke had not, you might say,

connected spiritually. O'Rourke just stood there, scratching his nose. Lee could be seen pulling up in front of the precinct entrance. Kennedy walked towards the swing door.

"By the way, I'll probably be over to see you later," O'Rourke hissed at Kennedy and then grumbled something else under his breath.

"What was that?" Kennedy did not look over his shoulder as he pushed his way out into the bitterly cold air.

"I said I always say what I mean."

Kennedy let the door swing behind him like a gunslinger in an old film set saloon.

Under ordinary circumstances the opulence of the Waldorf would have been delightful and he would have given room service some serious hammering. But these were not ordinary circumstances and Kennedy's appetite had disappeared like the morning mist. The same could not be said for his desire to sleep. He tipped the bell boy for helping him with his pathetic little bag, and sat down on the soft quilted bed. No sooner had he sat down than his shoulders began to droop, then his head, and he was off to the land of nod. He would probably have slept like that for two days but some hours later he was rudely awoken by a call from reception. O'Rourke was downstairs.

"Tell him to wait, I'll be down in twenty minutes." Kennedy rubbed his head and shoulders. Felt like he'd been sat on by a sumo wrestler. A hot shower helped revive him, then he slipped into his trousers. They looked like they had been crushed by a motorway cement mixer and the shirt, when he finally managed to get into it, resembled something which had been tied into a small ball for three or four years. He was a sartorial disaster, but there was nothing he could do. He let himself out of the room, closing the solid teak door behind him. The silent lift propelled him down to the foyer, where O'Rourke was waiting—crisp, showered, and shaved. He made Kennedy look like a river rat.

"There was no need to dress up," O'Rourke quipped. Couldn't waste an opportunity to get one in. He looked Kennedy up and down, then stared at his shoes, which had been polished once, a long time ago. Kennedy was about to say something when he remembered something which hit him like a lightening bolt. He turned back to the lift, summoned it, and went back up to his room leaving O'Rourke standing there with his mouth open.

Kennedy hadn't phoned Beverley! She still had no idea what had happened unless Maxim had contacted her, but why would he? He sat down on the oversoft bed and punched in the dialling code for England. He checked his watch. It would be three in the afternoon there. He would just catch her before she went to get Milly. He got the answer machine and started to leave a message when a breathless Beverley snatched the phone up. She'd been answering the call of nature when he'd rung. She'd been anxious, otherwise she'd have left it. On his other trips he would always phone when he arrived.

Beverley was stricken when he told her everything which had happened. He left out the bit about the bridge. There was enough there to be getting on with. She cried some tears, he reassured her, and she listened and cried some more. He told her about O'Rourke and he promised to phone her later once the disagreeable American had gone. Then he told her he loved her and went back to rejoin a most irritated and upset O'Rourke, in the foyer.

<u>16</u>

Beverley put the phone down and dialled Ray's mobile straight away. She wanted to talk to him. He didn't like being kept in the dark about anything. He listened until Beverley had finished telling the tale.

"Keep me up to date, sis."

"Yeah, course." She put the phone down and rubbed her brow. She had a kingsized headache coming on. Rex trotted up and nuzzled her. He always seemed to know when she was feeling poorly.

Across the river, Ray stood looking out of his window. It gave him a great view of the common where he let his two Japanese hunting dogs run. He loved his dogs. They were massive and originally bred for bear hunting. He kept them in a big purpose built kennel at the back of his garden. He could hear them bark as he picked up his phone and dialled Lex's number.

"Yol." Lex always answered the phone in the same way.

"It's Ray, man. Can you get hold of Ice, Eyeball and Big Lip?"

"No problem." Lex did not waste words.

"Good." He put the phone down and went out to the garden to feed the dogs. The grey clouds in the South London sky told him it was about to rain.

17

"Sorry, had to make a phone call," Kennedy said as he sat down in the beautiful leather seat opposite O'Rourke.

A few "B-list" movie stars wandered around the foyer waiting to receive recognition therapy. They were joined by a few "A-list" ones, who were less in need of therapy and more in need of a room.

"Don't mind me, I have nothing better to do than stand around waiting on you," O'Rourke spat.

"You really are a nasty piece of work, aren't you." Kennedy brought no humour into his voice. There wasn't meant to be any.

"It's this work and this precinct. It would touch anyone," he said quite quietly.

"Yes, but that doesn't explain your rudeness. Like the way you spoke to Officer..." Kennedy tried to remember the young Chinese American's name. It escaped him, must be the stress of the last day or so.

"Blinker." O'Rourke licked his lips as he summoned the waiter over to them. Kennedy shook his head in sadness.

"There you go. Why is that necessary?"

"What?" O'Rourke ignored the waiter who had come over immediately after he was summoned.

"The nickname for him. What's wrong with his real name?"

O'Rourke seemed to ignore that question.

"What do you want to drink?"

"Miller, please, Miller Lite." He felt like a nice cold beer.

O'Rourke signalled that they would have two of them. The waiter treated them as though they had ordered vintage champagne. That was class. They were in the Waldorf and therefore they would be treated the same as Sultans or Kings—the mark of a truly great hotel. It was a theme which was dear to O'Rourke's heart. Class and style. He considered himself something of an authority on the subject.

Look around you, what do you see?" He gave an almost regal wave of the hand. Kennedy did as he asked. He frowned and shook his head. He saw smartly dressed New Yorkers, city brokers, movie stars or at least people who looked like them and of course the beautiful decor.

"A nice hotel," he said with some understatement.

"Is that all?" O'Rourke seemed disappointed.

"You're a Brit. I thought you understood things like this. It's not just a hotel, it's more than that." The waiter returned with the beer. O'Rourke helped himself and took a deep long swig of the Miller. It hit the spot like a massage from a six handed maiden. "It's a piece of history, an example of real class, breeding." He looked slightly obsessive when he said this. He took another swig of Miller.

"Class. I see." Kennedy wasn't sure where this was leading but he didn't feel comfortable. He also took a drink from his bottle of beer, looking self-consciously out of one eye at the waiter, who smiled back. Even if he disapproved of drinking from the bottle, which he did, he would never have shown it.

"Is that why you think I understand class? Because I'm a Brit?"

"The point is that Blinker.." O'Rourke couldn't finish, as Kennedy interrupted him.

"You mean, Lee."

"Whatever. The fact is Chinese, African, you name it, they don't understand class." O'Rourke looked pleased with himself and took another drink from his bottle in celebration.

Kennedy imagined O'Rourke with an eyepatch, bandana and callouses on his fingers from playing too much dixie on the banjo. "I don't think that's true. Anyway, it's different between Britain and the United States." Kennedy took a drink from the bottle.

"How is it different? You're either from the right class or you're not."

"In Europe you can look at social stratification in relation to class, and Marxist analysis can be applied to the social systems of the United Kingdom and Europe," explained Kennedy. His eyes narrowed, O'Rourke certainly was a nasty piece of work on some subjects. He finished the last of his beer, unable to hide his discomfort.

"Something wrong?"

You, thought Kennedy. "I'm feeling sore," he said nursing his bruised shoulder. It really had been a rough last twenty four hours. Despite the conversation, he couldn't get the violin out of his mind. Such a precious instrument, and he had let it get away from him. He felt almost overwhelmed with self-loathing.

"And how is it different in America?" O'Rourke sniffed. He barely understood a word of what Kennedy had already said. Clearly he was a more educated man than himself, and that was enough to make his colon itch with irritation. But still, he was curious.

"Well," Kennedy welcomed the distraction, he needed to try to get his mind off of all the shit that was getting him down, "...America is made up of groups. In groups and out groups. Unlike the class structure in Europe, here in the States, you can move from one group to another, by having more money. Money is the key to social movement. Whereas in Europe money can't affect any movement one way or another through the social classes."

The waiter returned, his brightly polished button reflecting the light from the impressive chandelier.

"Two more beers," O'Rourke said gruffly. The waiter

glided away as though he was on castors.

"Basically it all adds up to a completely different way of life. Americans are optimistic because there's a point to believing you can do better." Kennedy was warming to his theme.

"In Britain we're pessimists, full of irony. I think the weather has got a lot to do with it." He folded his arms as though he had just delivered a sermon. He could be a bit pompous, when he wanted. "By the way," Kennedy began, "...irony's not a food supplement."

O'Rourke tilted his head to one side and sucked his teeth. There was a moment of silence between them.

"What if I didn't want one?" Kennedy asked.

"One what?"

"Beer."

The sounds of New York forced their way into the hotel, cutting through the rising tension between them.

"Then I'd drink it myself," O'Rourke answered coldly.

They did not like each other. That much was clear. It was not helped by the fact that whilst O'Rourke understood little of what Kennedy had said initially, he didn't have a clue about the second part. It really pissed him off. He steered the conversation back to the bundle at the airport and Caruso's corruption. On that ground, at least, he felt safe.

"We didn't know about Caruso. Not a clue." O'Rourke shook his head.

Kennedy watched the waiter, going effortlessly about his business in the distance, before taking a deep breath. "I lost a lot last night. I nearly didn't get through it alive. What was all that? Caruso, I mean." He rubbed his eyes.

The bright buttoned waiter returned with the beers. O'Rourke took a drink from his and almost immediately regretted it. That's the trouble with alcohol. You're drinking with someone else and before long you stop thinking about whether or not you actually want the booze and ordering becomes more of a reflex. Kennedy asked the waiter to bring some herbal tea. He took pity on the man and drew the line at asking for black horehound. That would have been a little bit too much, even for the Waldorf Astoria.

As though on cue, Lee arrived in the foyer. Smiling as always, he strode over to the two men with as much purpose as he could muster.

"Hello Mister Kennedy, Sir." The second part of his sentence was aimed at O'Rourke which stifled his look of disapproval.

"We were just discussing Caruso and how he went sour," O'Rourke said somewhat inaccurately. Lee nodded and sat down. He adjusted the cuffs of his shirt, although they didn't really need sorting. It was more nervous energy than anything else; he felt unsteady in O'Rourke's company. He felt relaxed around the Londoner though, and found him genuine. There was also something sad about him which touched a nerve in Lee. There was an element to Kennedy which generated sympathy, not pity, just a feeling that there was a lot of hurt going on under the man's skin.

"There's no telling how these things happen," Lee said, shaking his head no to the waiter who had come back to take his order. Kennedy took a drink of his herbal tea. He'd tasted better, but then this was America. They were a bit unsure when it came to making proper tea.

"Lee was going to take you round Chinatown tonight. Give you a look before you go tomorrow." He glanced at Lee, privately wishing Lee could lose Kennedy in Chinatown. Not a difficult task.

Lee stood up. "I'll come back for you at nine Mr Kennedy?" He had finished adjusting his shirt cuffs. Kennedy looked up at him.

"Do I have a choice?" He asked with no humour and a straight face. Not difficult for Londoners, when they put their mind to it.

"With me you always have a choice." Lee answered. O'Rourke had little patience for this. It sounded like twenty questions on a cheap quiz show.

"It's the most useful thing you could do tonight, apart from run up a room service bill. Seems to me you've cost the Frenchman enough already." It was a vicious and cheap shot but it hit a note with Kennedy which was not of the musical kind.

"Of course you could always have a meal with Mr Laffe. I'm sure the orchestra will pick up the tab." O'Rourke was warming to his comedy routine, especially as he could plainly see it was getting to Kennedy. Lee stood there blinking a couple of times. He felt sorry for Kennedy.

"I'll meet you down here at nine," Kennedy told Lee over his aching shoulder as he walked past.

"See you later," he said to O'Rourke without turning round.

"Not if I see you first," O'Rourke answered. He was thrilled at seeing the back of both the Brit and the Chinaman. He gulped the last of the beer as the smile faded from his face. The waiter presented him with the bill. Waldorf prices plus fifteen per cent tax. O'Rourke's sense of humour evaporated faster than snow on the first day of summer.

18

Lee and Kennedy went out into the night air. The wind was down and there was a light snow falling. Another night Kennedy would have enjoyed the atmosphere in New York. Tonight, however was another matter. They walked to Lee's car which was parked some distance away. A late model Oldsmobile. The leather seats felt comfortable, as Kennedy slipped in on the passenger's side. He made the compulsory mistake of going to the driver's side first. Common enough, and less dangerous than driving down the wrong side of the street.

Lee blinked so frequently it seemed like more than just a nervous thing. He caught Kennedy looking at him as he selected drive and eased the car out. Kennedy felt a bit awkward as it had been obvious what had been going through his mind. Lee grinned as he slipped the car into the busy Manhattan street.

"I hope they have a happier Christmas than the one I'm going to have," Kennedy said as they drove along quite slowly.

"They don't say Happy Christmas here, you know." He looked sideways at Kennedy and yes, blinked.

"So what should I say?" Kennedy looked out of the window as Manhattan shimmied rather than flashed past. Lee had rejoined Park Avenue and was nearly at Astor Place.

"Happy Holidays. Means no one gets offended." He smiled to himself as they drove through Astor Place. O'Rourke would feel at home here, Kennedy thought. Any square which sounded as though it was named after a rich mover and shaker, or socialite of the century, would have a special place in his heart. He wondered if it was connected in any way to the Lady Astor of his history books.

"Lady Astor had a place in England, Cliveden. It was where the Profumo thing happened." Kennedy knew as soon as he said it that he was reaching for a piece of English history which would probably not have a place in Lee's heart. He was right. A complete look of disinterest was plastered all over the driver's face. There was no point trying to explain a government minister and Christine Keeler to someone stone cold. Too much hassle, so he brought the conversation back to the previous subject.

"It's important to you that people don't get offended?"

The traffic had eased and Lee had made good progress. They turned into Confucius Plaza and Lee stopped the car in a parking bay. He kissed his teeth. More Jamaican than Chinese, but this was New York, anything goes.

"Isn't it important to you?" Lee gave him a sideways glance.

"Sure it matters to me. It just seems that you can get a bit too precise sometimes." Kennedy shrugged his shoulders.

"Precise?" Lee spat. He kissed his teeth again and blinked. He put the car in park, pulled the key from the ignition, and got out of the car more quickly than was necessary.

Kennedy got out as well and stood there. There was an evil wind blowing now. Coming in sharp from the East River, it had lasered its way through the grid of New York's streets. He turned his collar up against its biting ferocity. It was a futile gesture. The wind increased, he grimaced against its edge. Lee walked around the back of the car, pulling on some rather spectacular winter gloves. Kennedy could tell they were fur lined, there was the tell-tale sign of white wispy bits coming out of the bottom.

Lee and Kennedy started walking into Chinatown, a heaving mass of humanity. It was almost inconceivable that so many people could live so close together and not go crazy. But then, of course, some people have no choice.

"Precise." Lee repeated with a slightly softer tone than a few moments ago. He waved his hands around as they walked. Faces peered out at them from dimly lit alleys leading to the back doors of restaurants, clubs and over-crowded homes.

Light flashed and reflected off the tepid water lying in the gutter. Steam rose from the drains.

"These people live by precise. Everything matters to them. How you do something, when you do it. You can't be too precise." Lee took a deep breath. It was obvious that it mattered to him, very much indeed. By now they were deep in Chinatown at the corner of Bayard and Mott. Far in the distance you could see the tiny outline of the Manhattan Bridge. Lee stopped walking and sat down on a large ornate seat. It was raining quite hard now but neither of them minded. In fact the rain was quite refreshing. The massive shape of a buddhist temple stood behind them.

Lee sighed and put his chin in his hands. Car lights danced off the temple walls and sent beams shafting into the night like millions of grains of rice.

"Chinatown has over 150,000 people in it. That's bigger than a small town. It is easy to get lost here or to disappear forever. Friends and enemies are never far away." He did not look at Kennedy, but he knew he was listening.

"I am sorry about the instrument you lost. Really. But there are more important things in life. People lose their lives or worse the lives of people whom they love above all else." His eyes misted over, he was deep in thought. Still he was not looking at Kennedy. He didn't have to, he knew his words were not landing on deaf ears.

He gestured behind him towards the temple. "There are twelve of these in Chinatown. They all mean something to someone."

"Right," said Kennedy. There was a time to talk and a time to listen. This was a time to listen.

"Everyone needs something to believe in. Hope is one of the most powerful life forces known to man. Don't you agree, Mr Kennedy?" Kennedy nodded.

"We all need hope, that's for sure." Kennedy felt his thoughts wander off to the time when he lost his. As if Lee knew, he changed his tone.

"The Snakehead gangs work off peoples' hopes and dreams. No-one stands a chance once they go on that journey. Only slavery awaits those who go. They are evil. All of them." He looked around at the temple as though he was looking for inspiration.

"They care about nothing except money and power." He sighed deeply as he thought about it.

"You have to be ruthless when you're dealing with them. You cut off one head and another one grows. The whole body must be dealt with if you're going to be successful against them." He shivered as the very thought of them made his blood run cold.

"Where do you fit in all this?" Kennedy was intrigued.

"The force needs some more Chinese faces to try to help out. That's all. The Chinese community keeps itself to itself. Always has. They need some more Orientals to point the way."

The sound of a fog horn from the East River interrupted Lee's monologue and Kennedy's thoughts. They looked at each other for a while.

"You're going tomorrow. It's the best thing. This is a dangerous place for you, Mister Kennedy. You're lucky to be alive as it is, after all. "

Kennedy nodded.

"I know I've never been much good at maths. Music was my thing. But a lot about all this doesn't add up. I know there are bent cops all over the place but why did Caruso show up last night?" He could feel his shoulders slump. He was very tired. His senses were flooded by the smell of stir fry from a nearby restaurant. He could see the mixture of human sweat and steam pouring out of the side door.

Lee looked in the same direction. "There's probably a dozen people in that place who came to the Golden Mountain thanks to the snakehead." He picked at a gap in his front tooth with the little finger of his right hand. Kennedy noticed the top, just above the knuckle was missing.

"What happened there?" He touched the finger with the index one of his own hand. Lee didn't seem to mind. He laughed. "People think I've been in trouble with the Yakuza."

"Yakuza?" Kennedy had heard the term before. But he wasn't quite sure. Knew it was something oriental.

"Japanese gangsters. Plenty of tradition. People can't tell the difference between Chinese and Japanese. We all look the same." Kennedy squinted at him.

"I see what you mean," he said with a smile. Lee looked taken aback for a moment then laughed.

"When you get it wrong with the Yakuza, you have to cut off the tip of your little finger of your right hand."

"Why?"

"To show humility and to compensate for something you may or may not have done," Lee said.

"So what happened to you?"

Lee licked his lips and looked serious for a moment.

"Deckchair. Trip to the beach when I was young. Been afraid of sand ever since. It has that kind of effect on you, believe me." He smiled at the end of his confession.

"It would, wouldn't it," Kennedy agreed.

"Not very dramatic, but the truth." Lee smiled.

"The truth often is pretty dull," Kennedy said. His thoughts wandered. There was something nagging at the back of his mind. Any further time for thought was brutally removed. The piercing whistle was just enough to give him warning. He started to dive for the ground, but it really was the aggressive shove from Lee that actually saved his life.

The reason for the noise was embedded in the tree just behind him and slightly above his right ear. He'd seen the knife before. Last time it had been stuck near his ear. He knew also that the tip could be the one laced with poison.

In the shadows, the quiet tune of Mastermind could be heard. Missing was getting to be a habit and it was pissing the psychopath off. He finished whistling his favourite tune and walked slowly over to the tree. Kennedy and Lee were long gone. He'd nearly gotten rid of that loose end tonight. He hated loose ends, they were not Chinese. Laffe, the man with the mouse in him, had told him all he needed to know. He'd been beside himself with rage when he'd found out that Kennedy was alive. It was bad enough that Little Dragon had chewed his backside over things not going precisely to plan. His continued prestige depended on him tidying things up.

Kennedy had to die. The sooner the better. As it was he couldn't believe that the drop onto the freeway hadn't killed him in the first place. Now this chance to take out the Englishman had gone. But only for the moment. There was little to protect him, particularly if that stupid looking policeman was all that stood between him and his fate. He pulled the still quivering blade out of the young sapling and placed it carefully back into the super fast sheath strapped to his upper arm. He had two of them, one on each. The blades were black and dull so they would not reflect light. The holsters had been specially made by a blind leathersmith in Macau. He remembered him well.

The product was very expensive and Pai-Lan had been very tempted not to pay him, but to kill him instead. He'd changed his mind when he realised just how good the old man was at Wing Chun. No-one ever prospered by making a foolish mistake. That day he knew that taking the old blind man on could have been risky. Pai-Lan was dangerous and he certainly enjoyed killing, but he prided himself on making the right decisions when they counted. He took a deep breath and closed his jacket over his expensive designer shirt. He looked at the general area where Lee and Kennedy had disappeared, and sighed. There would be another time, soon. He knew that deep in his soul. The tune to Mastermind came easily back to his lips. One of the few muggers still left in New York stepped out of the shadows, looking for some easy pickings. He saw the deranged look on Pai-Lan's face and swiftly changed his mind. He would never know how close he had come to losing his greasy little life. One of the knives had already been in Pai-Lan's hand ready for its soft fleshy target.

Lee and Kennedy only stopped running when Kennedy held his hand out and touched Lee on the arm. He couldn't run another inch. His heart felt like it was going to pop.

"Your friend from the bridge, I think. He looked back in the darkness from where they had just run." He was breathing hard but not wheezing like Kennedy. Kennedy wiped the sweat and grime from his face. This type of encounter was becoming a habit he could well do without. What did they think he still had? The violin didn't come with a bow.

"Come on. Let's get back to the hotel. That's enough for one night. Besides I have to phone this one in." Lee stood up from the grass and wiped himself down.

"Do you have family?" Kennedy asked as he regained his feet. Lee blinked in the darkness.

"Yes," he said matter-of-factly. Kennedy waited for him to continue. He would have had a long wait, if he hadn't spoken again.

"And?"

"And what?" Lee answered. If he was irritated, he didn't show it.

"How many and where are they?"

"I never talk about my family. Never." The first bit had a friendly tone but the last word was spat like a shard of steel. Kennedy knew that any further discussion was not to be considered. The subject was closed.

They walked the few minutes back to the car in silence. There wasn't far to go as they had already run some distance back towards Confucius Plaza.

Lee phoned in the incident on the car radio and then dropped Kennedy off at the hotel. It was probably just as well that he was going back tomorrow. There was a uniformed officer already at the hotel when he got there. He would be staying the night to make sure there wasn't a repeat of Pai-Lan's activities. O'Rourke had arranged it, he did not want a dead Brit on his hands. He had enough of a headache with a bent cop and dead bodies piling up. The officer did not look like he was complaining, a night in the Waldorf was a treat.

19

Kennedy made sure the adjoining door was unlocked as the officer was staying in the room next door. He did not want to die, not yet. He still had a daughter to bring up. Sleep came easy and it wasn't long before he was in the land of nod. The morning light was streaming into the hotel room before he knew it. Some muffins and eggs over easy, made the day ahead seem an easier prospect. Time went quickly and he put his few belongings together and was ready for the police car when it met him at the front of the hotel. He'd spent a few minutes reading The New York Times while waiting in the foyer. The front page told the story of the Snakehead activities and the kidnapping of Ka-Lut. She was very young and very pretty. She could only have been nineteen or twenty in the picture. The story under the photograph speculated about who could have been responsible for her kidnapping and why. No contact had been made by the abductors who had snatched the young girl seemingly without warning. She was about to start studying at the school of music in New York. Kennedy noted with not a little sense of irony, that her musical instrument was the violin. She was very good at it, by all accounts. A very promising student, whereabouts unknown. The paper stopped short of actually saying it, but they hinted that no-one actually knew whether she was dead or alive.

There were two surprises in store for him that morning. The first was that O'Rourke was in the car which came to pick him up. The truth was that O'Rourke couldn't wait to get rid of him and came along to make sure everything went smoothly. The second was that when they arrived at JFK, Beverley was there. She cried when she saw him. When she finished holding him close and telling him she loved him he was able to speak.

"How did you get here?" He knew it was a stupid question as soon as he said it. Her eyebrows raised like Tower Bridge at dawn.

"I flew." She smiled.

"You know what I meant." Kennedy was really pleased to see her but he was not in the mood for arsing around.

"I managed to get a cheap flight. Intertravel, dotty. com, or whatever it was. I'm on the flight back to Paris with you." She held him close to her. She knew that coming was the right thing to do. He allowed her to hold him but he was not at ease. There was so much going on. She felt his distance and stood back.

"There's something I have to do," he said as he gave her his hand luggage. Under different circumstances she would probably have dumped his bags in the nearest bin. She had not come all this way to be treated like a redcap. She half expected him to tip her when he returned. She bit her lip and tried to hide her resentment at this treatment. She did not do a very good job. Kennedy went over to the phones, slowly. It had been an exhausting few days and it was beginning to take its toll.

He punched in the numbers for the New York City symphony orchestra. A woman with perfect pitch answered the phone.

"Is Mr Latte there?" He knew as soon as he said it that he had got the name wrong.

"I'm sorry?"

"Forgive me. Laffe, not Latte," he said with a smile she could not possibly see.

"I'm sorry, sir." She sounded nothing of the sort. That's the thing about perfect pitch. You can't lie, as the slightest change in tone sticks out.

Kennedy knew what was coming next.

"There is no Mister Laffe here. No-one of that name is connected to the orchestra." She sounded quite sure so there seemed little point in asking her if she was.

"Who is the gentleman in charge of the orchestra's affairs?" That was a mistake. He wasn't thinking straight. There was a definite freeze on the end of the phone. Winter on the Hudson, make no mistake.

"There is no gentleman, as you put it, in charge of the affairs of our organisation. It is a lady." Her reply was icy. There seemed little point in asking what her name was, the person who had come to see him at the precinct was definitely not of the female variety. What could this mean? The guy must have been an imposter. More than that, he probably led the knifeman to them last night. He and Lee had probably been followed all the way from the hotel. He shook his head, exasperated with himself. He should have known. The shoes. Laffe, Latte or whatever his name was, had scruffy shoes. Looked like they'd been worn in a particularly filthy marathon. No self-respecting professional New Yorker would go out with dirty shoes. That was for Brits. Even Kennedy had to admit that when it came to sartorial elegance the English were left behind by the Americans. His life could have depended on him remembering that.

These people obviously had fingers in every rotten nook and cranny either side of the Atlantic. Seemed like a good time to leave Stateside well alone. He didn't say anything to Beverley when he returned. She was standing by the same spot but his bag was pointedly sitting on the floor in a rather dusty patch. That, and the look on her face told him something was up. He knew it was a reaction to the way he had greeted her but there was nothing he could do, or felt like doing now.

20

They checked in for their flight back to Paris. Kennedy was looking forward to seeing Maxim and apologising in person. The flight passed without incident and Beverley and Kennedy got a taxi straight away at Charles de Gaulle. They both had that overnight traveller smell but neither cared. Maxim's was the next destination. He was there in his dusty workshop, looking like a smile was the thing of the past. He hardly looked at Kennedy as he listened to his tale of woe, the loss of the violin and the murder and mayhem in the Big Apple.

"Who could have known?" Kennedy had been wondering about this all along. The Amati had not been stolen by accident. It had been a pre-arranged job. Smooth, efficient by his standards if not the Snakehead. Different approaches and completely opposite priorities. Beverley sat in the corner of the workshop sipping a glass of ice cold mineral water as the men talked but did not look at each other. Maxim was taking it really bad. He could not look at Kennedy and the atmosphere was sharp and brittle like the first ice of a Peter Pan winter. Maxim shrugged his shoulders at Kennedy's question. Kennedy felt stupid as soon as he had asked it.

If Maxim had any ideas he would hardly be standing there discussing it; he would be straight to the police to get the damn violin back, surely.

"It was owned by a little old lady in Sussex. Like something from a storybook. Small cottage near Haywards Heath. Lived there all her life." Maxim's voice was tense and strained. He also sounded incredibly sorry for himself.

"She doesn't know yet. She doesn't have a phone so I can't break the news. She rarely lets that instrument go, and this happens."

"It was in the paper in New York. Surely she knows by now," Kennedy said.

"She doesn't read papers. Doesn't own a television, I don't know anything else about her. You can be fairly certain she won't have read it on the internet." The last part of his sentence was heavy with sarcasm. It did not suit the Frenchman.

"You lost it, you can tell her." His tone was not one of request but an order. It sounded almost military in the way he said it. Kennedy thought for a few moments.

"Okay. Give me her address and I'll go straight there when I get back to England." Maxim scribbled something down on the back of an old music paper and handed it to Kennedy.

"I'll call you when I've seen her," Kennedy said. Maxim did not reply but started to clean a flute which was lying in pieces on his workbench in front of him. It was time for Beverley and Kennedy to leave. It was a subdued and quiet trip back to the airport. Raoul was not around to take them back to Charles de Gaulle, so it seemed wise not to ask. Anyway, Kennedy didn't feel like getting a lift; he was in the mood for a taxi.

They boarded the plane in silence. They were somewhere across the North sea when Beverley punctured the quiet between them.

"What are you going to do when you get back?"

"First, I'll go to this address Maxim gave me then I'll figure out what's next. There's still an awful lot about this which doesn't add up."

"Nothing adds up unless you look at it in the right order," Beverley said. She was still in a foul mood. The journey had not been helped by the treatment she had received at the hands of French customs when they had landed from New York. They had treated her like a piece of dirt. Seemed to think she was on the game. She knew it was just because she was black. France was not her favourite country. For goodness sake, she'd even heard they'd banned some people of colour using their bloody sports centres in Marseilles. What a country. That Kennedy looked like a week old turd had not helped matters. They thought at first he was her pimp.

<u>21</u>

There was a surprise waiting for Kennedy at Heathrow. Ray stood at Arrivals, his legs shoulder width apart and his hands on his hips. He was flanked by Lex and another guy Kennedy had never seen before.

"Sis." Ray embraced his sister. The look he gave Kennedy was cold and what he said was to the point.

"What shit you got my sister into?" Kennedy did not need this.

"It's got nothing to do with you." Wrong choice of words. Ray took a step forward. It was clear he was not about to give Kennedy a welcoming hug, far from it. Beverley stepped between them.

"No Ray." He stood there for a few moments, though to Kennedy it seemed like an age, then he appeared to relax a bit.

"Ice, get the bags." He didn't take his eyes off Kennedy as he spoke to the large black guy dripping with diamonds. He had enough in his ears, round his neck and on his hands to fill a Bond Street jewellery shop. Way over the top. It was unlikely anyone had ever told him to tone it down. Ice was a hard, lonely man, with few friends. He only took orders from Ray. The bredrin had helped him many years ago when it looked like he was going to be cut into small pieces and stored in a meat packing warehouse in Romford. The sound of a chainsaw still made him freeze.

"Bev, you better go with him. He doesn't know which bags are yours. We'll wait here." Beverley hesitated until Ray gave her a small smile.

"It's alright. I won't hurt him." She headed off in the direction of the luggage carrousel so she didn't hear him mutter under his breath.

"For now."

Kennedy did though.

"Look. None of this has got anything to do with your sister, or you." The second part of his sentence sounded a lot braver than he felt. Ray looked at him out of the corner of his eye.

"Everything that happens to you touches my sister and anything which touches my sister is my business, end of story," he sniffed.

Kennedy sighed. This was not a discussion which seemed to have any room for compromise. He had to look on the bright side. He was still walking and in possession of all his faculties. Ray was not a man who usually discussed verbally anyway. He kept his powers of persuasion wrapped in dust clothes in the boot of the Lexus.

"So what happened?" Ray now had both of his eyes trained on him.

Kennedy told him the whole sorry tale. He was still talking from the back seat of the Lexus as it threaded its way down the M4 back to London, closely followed by a silver Merc containing Ray's two other soldiers, Eyeball and Big Lip. They both had quite obvious physical characteristics which supported their names. They shared one thing in common, experience in the psychiatric wing of the local hospital. If it were not for an overworked and underfunded system they would probably still have been on the day wing munching scrambled egg on toast and watching re-runs of Crossroads on daytime telly. The whole entourage dropped Beverley and Kennedy off at Kennedy's house, though there was some persuading to be done before Ray would leave his sister behind. His parting words,"I'll not be far away," were not only meant for his sister.

Beverley went straight round to collect Milly from Cordelia's where she had been staying. She knew that Murray wouldn't mind, as the little one had stayed with her many times. Kennedy was in the kitchen cleaning his cup of the last dregs of coffee when a pair of arms wrapped themselves around his neck.

"Daddy, you smell nice." Milly was sweet. She would say he smelt nice even if he'd been working in a sewer for a month. Daughters never can see anything wrong with their dads. Just something about the bond. Different when it came to mothers.

He knelt down and whispered gently in her ear, "How's my favourite girl?" He smiled.

"I'm nobody, Daddy." The smile froze on his face.

22

There wasn't really any time to waste. It was hardly an hour before he was in the back of the Lexus again and heading south through London, for Sussex. Beverley wanted to come but someone had to look after Milly, and Cordelia was busy. Ray left Big Lip and Ice to keep watch on Kennedy's house from the confines of Ice's customised BMW complete with metallic paint and low profile tyres. Kennedy thought that with the name Eyeball he was best suited to the task, but after careful consideration he decided to keep this thought to himself. He had no wish to push his luck.

The weather was its usual British self: dark clouds, light rain, shadows like the hellriders of the storm. No wonder the Brits always seemed so obsessed with the weather. It was, at times, supernatural. It demanded attention, the way it so dominated every sphere of life. Kennedy was scrunched low in the back of the car beside Eyeball. Lex was driving with Ray in the front seat. Despite the impressive width of the Lexus, there was precious little room for Kennedy. Eyeball was clearly packing more than just his muscles. Kennedy had wanted to come alone but that had not been possible or even open to discussion. The boys were supposed to be on his side but somehow that didn't make him feel any better. Lex slowed down for the turning off for Haywards Heath. He wasn't a very good driver but he tried his best. Even with practice his driving had not really improved. In fact, it had gone downhill. It had a lot to do with his concentration, or lack thereof. You would have thought that with his ability to focus in dicey situations, he'd be a more skillful driver, but he wasn't.

They followed the directions Maxim had given Kennedy and finally found themselves driving quite slowly up a tight winding country lane. Signs and Maxim's crumpled instructions guided them to the quaintly named Rose Cottage. They pulled up in the gravel drive. Kennedy loved that sound of scrunching under the wheels, it made him nostalgic and brought him back to schooldays—a warm and comfortable feeling.

A little old lady suddenly appeared behind him as he closed the door with a thunk. She looked happy enough, but that would soon change.

"Good afternoon. My name's Mister Kennedy. I've come to see you Miss Turner." He walked slowly towards her.

"Aren't you going to lock your car, Mister Kennedy? There's been a lot of theft here recently. I would be dreadfully upset if anything was to happen to your property."

"It's alright." He gestured at the unsmiling faces of the men in the car. She obviously hadn't seen them.

"Oh. Would your friends like a cup of tea?"

"It's alright. I don't think they drink tea."

She stood to one side and gestured for Kennedy to enter her little dwelling. Kennedy walked forward then froze. He was confronted with one of his worst nightmares. It wasn't that he didn't like cats, it was more that he couldn't stand them and was extremely allergic. There wasn't one, but three of them waiting to greet him inside the cottage. Miss Turner saw him hesitate.

"Don't worry Mister Kennedy. My babies won't harm you, they love meeting new people. He smiled the empty cold smile of someone who has no choice. If his constant sneezing bothered Miss Turner, then she didn't show it. Instead, she took great delight in introducing the furry nightmare to him one by one. Kennedy's eyes were streaming. Miss Turner would probably have shown some concern if she could have seen Kennedy. Her spectacles were made of glass as thick as the bottoms of old jam jars. It became clear why the little old lady had not seen the guys in the car.

"That's Tiddles," said Miss Turner pointing to one of the cats.

"And that's Diddles," she said pointing at the same cat. They shuffled around a bit then she pointed yet again at the same feline creature. She couldn't tell the difference.

"And that is Piddles." She laughed at the last name.

"I called him that because he does rather naughty things on the carpet. It gets worse in the cold." The last bit was more than he needed to know. Judging by the state of the carpet it did not get very warm in this part of England.

Ignoring the cats, Kennedy took a look at the little old lady who had sat herself directly across from him. He doubted that she could see him, her eyesight appeared to be so dreadful. Her face looked like it was fighting to get to the front. She had wisps of grey hair cut neatly and small pointed ears which sat either side of a pleasant, gentle face. She looked like a little old lady who appears on television commercials advertising supermarket deals. The hat stand with something resembling a tea cosy on it, in the corner, told Kennedy what she would wear if she ever ventured out. She quickly answered Kennedy's thought.

"I don't get out very often. My babies keep me company. Without them, I suspect I would probably go mad." She fixed Kennedy with a strange distant look which suggested her mind had wandered for a moment. It looked as though her little family had failed rather miserably in making sure Miss Turner had not already checked out from reality. Then, all of a sudden, she was back with him.

"How rude of me, Mister Kennedy."

"I'm sorry?" Kennedy didn't think she had been rude to him. She didn't seem at all capable.

"I haven't offered you a cup of tea."

Kennedy looked around him quickly. It did not seem that any part of the house was out of bounds to the hairy horrors. That probably included the cups in the kitchen. He shook his head in total earnest.

"No thank-you, really."

She stood up. "Well, you won't mind if I make one for myself." She was gone into the kitchen before he could object. Not that he would have, of course. She banged around for a while, then the noise of a whistle told him that her brew was ready. He kicked one of the cats away from him. It made a noise which thankfully she did not hear. She came back in carrying a small tray. She laid it down on a little table in front of her. Then Kennedy realised his mistake. It wasn't a hat, it was a tea cosy. She retrieved it from the hat stand and plonked it down over the small china teapot painted with little birds. They reminded him of the little swallows tattooed on the bloody hands of the man who had nearly murdered him.

She poured some milk into her cup, then sat back and looked directly at Kennedy. He doubted that she could actually see him. He wasn't doing much better, his eyes were streaming.

"What can I do for you, Mister Kennedy?" He forgot that little old ladies could be direct when they wanted to be.

"I should tell you that I've got bad news, Miss Turner." He hesitated before continuing.

"Mister Kennedy, you don't think I got to this age without hearing bad news before."

He took a deep breath.

"I was the man who was responsible for transporting your violin."

"It isn't mine. It's Teddy's." She interrupted him.
"Who's Teddy?"
"My husband."
"Where is he? I thought you lived alone." The last part of his sentence sounded rude although it wasn't supposed to. He winced at his own directness. It was unlike him. Maybe it was because he was finding it very difficult. He felt guilty. Another loss, another accident which he felt he should have been able to prevent or at least do something about. But he couldn't, not now anyway.

"He's in the kitchen. I'll get him." This took Kennedy aback. He had not been aware of anyone else in the cottage besides the two of them. This would prove interesting. Miss Turner returned with a large urn. She stood there, like a proud gardener with a prize courgette which had exceeded all reasonable expectations.

"Do you like it. I picked it from a catalogue. The original one was so ... well, dreary and Teddy always liked a bit of colour in his life." Kennedy waited for her to put her husband's cremated remains down on the hefty table. He did not want to tell her about the violin whilst she was holding her husband. The consequences could have been very unpleasant indeed, not to mention messy.

"Miss Turner, your violin has been stolen." He waited a few beats for it to sink in before finishing his sentence. "I am so sorry." The little old woman looked distracted for a moment then stood up. She was flustered and clearly very upset.

"Oh dear, I don't know what to do. What will Teddy say?" Kennedy hoped that Teddy would have nothing to say on the matter. Any speech coming from the urn would have rounded a crap week off with spectacular results.

She blinked back some tears then sat down again. Her shoulders slumped in resignation. "It's not me you know, it's Teddy. I knew I shouldn't have let it out like that, but the money comes in so handy you know."

"Yeah, I know."

Miss Turner fixed him with a sad gaze. She had very pretty eyes. It's funny how the eyes never age, in someone of spirit.

"You think I'm a mad old girl. don't you?"

"No, Miss Turner, I don't." Kennedy's voice was gentle and quiet. He was telling the truth. He didn't. Her next words cut him to the quick like the wind across the desert.

"You know. Just because someone's died doesn't mean the relationship ends. It never dies with them, you know.

"I know." And he did.

The same dark clouds were all over the sky when they drove back to central London. He'd explained everything to her without making it too gory, until she made it clear that she wanted the gore. What was a story without all the detail, she'd said.

Kennedy knew that the real thing of value in her life, all her life, was in the ceramic urn on the oversize table in her front room. A piece of wood with catgut, made by some obscure Maltese violin maker, was not the thing of her life. Even if strangers, men and women she'd never met, had said it was worth a lot of money.

23

They pulled up at a service station. Ray was hungry and Lex needed a piss. His bladder was straining to breaking point and his trousers felt as though they were ready to burst. This didn't help his already erratic driving. He parked the car outside the two white lines and at an awkward angle. Eyeball opened the door and leaned out.

"Can't you park a fuckin' motor, guy?"

"Nuthin' wrong with my parking." Lex's tone was less friendly. It was lost on Eyeball.

"Not surprising you got no kids. You must fuck like you park."

Lex got out of the car and flung the keys at Eyeball who exited the car at the same time. He caught them even though they were flying at a rate of knots.

"You fuckin' drive then."

Ray and Murray were out of the car by now. Ray nodded in the direction of Happy Jack's. It was the motorway eaterie's seventeenth name change in as many months.

"Come on, they'll catch up."

"If they don't kill each other first," Murray said as he looked over his shoulder half expecting to see only one left standing.

"You don't like conflict, do you?" Ray went in the double doors first. He didn't hold them open for Murray who only just caught them before they banged him full in the face.

"Some of us do manage to live our lives without it, you know."

Ray stopped and turned to face Murray. "That's easy when you lead soft rich lives, never getting off your arse."

"Like, you'd know." Murray looked braver than he felt.

Behind them Eyeball and Lex came through the doors and headed for the gents.

"I know a lot of things." His hard eyes were unblinking. Kennedy found it very hard to keep eye contact with him.

"Yeah right," was the best he could muster before he looked away.

Ray was right. He didn't do the conflict thing very well. Ray turned and headed into the food hall. Once again, he didn't bother to hold the doors open, but this time Murray was ready for him and caught them. Eyeball and Lex seemed to have resolved their differences by the time they sat down at the table, with Ray and Murray. They'd gotten themselves a couple of cokes. Lex drank his out of a straw, he didn't like the way they cleaned their glasses. Eyeball wasn't so fussy, most of his had been inhaled by the time they'd paid for them. Strains of Madness came over the tannoy.

"You'd think they'd mix it up a little." Ray nursed the mineral water which was standing next to the ham sandwich in front of him.

"Sorry?" Kennedy stirred his coffee. He avoided motorway tea. It was just too much like drainwater.

"It's always the same music at these places. They were playing Madness in the eighties." He took a sip of his water.

"Some things never change." Kennedy kept stirring his coffee. The milk was a bit lumpy.

"Certain things have to change." Ray took a sip from his glass.

"What do you mean?" There was a nasty taste in Kennedy's mouth. It was not the coffee.

"You and Beverley." Ray was to the point, but then you

can be when you're a bad bwoy from south of the river.

Kennedy sighed and stirred his coffee, even though he'd done it already.

"I'm not fucking about here. If it was up to me, you and her would never have been."

"Well, it's not up to you."

Lex and Eyeball were comparing their glasses and respective levels of cleanliness. Madness was still pumping out of the economy sound system.

"All I care about is Beverley. I turn my back and you're dragging her into all sorts of dangerous shit."

"I'm not dragging her anywhere." This was not turning into a very comfortable conversation. Ray leaned forward, his eyes told Kennedy what he was about to say before he even said it.

"I'm not joking."

"I'm not laughing."

Kennedy regretted it as soon as he said it. The hand around his throat contributed to that, in no small way. Ray licked his lips as his fingers tightened round Kennedy's windpipe. He had a grip like a cobra on speed. Kennedy didn't say anything else. He couldn't. It was Lex who came to his rescue, the straw still in his mouth. He put a hand on the piece of ripped steel posing as an arm which was still choking the breath out of Kennedy's body.

"Steady, man."

It was enough. Ray let his grip loosen and Kennedy sucked in a great gulp of air. Anymore discussion was going to have wait. Their table was surrounded by eight skinheads and a couple of others who had full heads of hair and some rather natty swastikas tattooed on their forearms. One of them had his face inches away from Ray's. The face was fleshy, rivulets of sweat ran down the several layers of skin which were once a single chin. Green eyes blazed hatred. If Ray was in the slightest bit intimidated he didn't show it.

"We don't like what you're doing to the white brother, brother."

Ray smiled. If fat Nazi had known him, he would have taken his face, in fact his whole body out of range. He didn't, so he didn't. Ray got the fat boy's testicles in one hand and squeezed and twisted at the same time. Kennedy winced. He had started to feel the power of Ray's grip himself, but now he could see the effect of its full range and hear the result. The man looked like he was going to burst out of his flying jacket as he let out a scream. It was cut short. Ray thrust his other hand, fingers stiff, open and straight into his windpipe, upending the skinhead. He still had hold of the testicles as he slammed the edge of his foot into his face. His face was split open from the corner of his mouth to his left ear. He was out of it, no more trouble was coming from him. Everything moved as though in slow motion. Eyeball produced a blade and sliced off a piece of another skinhead's ear. Lex was up and sidekicked another clean across the room. His victim was the biggest one and looked like he was going to come back for more, but he staggered unsteadily to his feet for a few moments then crumpled to the floor, but not before he had deposited the steak and kidney pie he'd had for his tea all over his Dr. Martens; nice too, eighteen eyelet, cherry red.

Half under the table, Ray grabbed Kennedy. The sweat off his arse had helped his inevitable slide to the floor. By now the law of mathematics had cut in. The other skinheads were not as brave as the ones who had taken the rough treatment. They clearly didn't want to know. Eyeball cleaned his blade on one of the men's Ben Sherman shirt as they exited the cafe. No-one had actually called the police yet as they were all in shock. Before he knew it, Kennedy was back in the Lexus and they were all heading back to London.

"Do you think we'll be pulled by the bluebottles?"

Eyeball said to no-one in particular.

"No. Everyone was too busy listening to the boy sing," Ray said. They all laughed except Kennedy who sat in the back seat, nursing his throat. He wasn't sure who scared him more— Ray, his bredrin, or the bastards who's tried to carve him up in New York. His thoughts wandered back to Miss Turner. He'd left her his number, even though she didn't have a phone. She'd touched a nerve inside him and he knew that he'd like to see the little old lady again.

24

Beverley was quiet when the three men dropped him off. She had her feet up on the sofa and appeared distant and distracted. He asked her if everything was alright and she just said it was her monthlies. So he didn't push. His throat was feeling better after Ray's unwanted attention and his appetite had come back. He made himself some sandwiches, ham with mustard and ham with mayonnaise, both on white. He would have fixed a more substantial meal but it was too late to eat too heavy.

He used to eat at all times of the day until Beverley pointed out that he shouldn't be having a main meal after six o'clock in the evening. The body turns it to fat and stores it. Then she told him that he shouldn't drink and eat at the same time. Both ask different things of the body which confuses it. You should eat, then drink or the other way around, not both at the same time. On top of that he'd started taking more vitamins which had also made a difference to his overall health. Vitamin D, E and C, the three main vitamins necessary for a healthy body. But there were no vitamins available for a broken heart. He knew that he was the same as Miss Turner. She carried the ashes around in an urn, he carried them around in his mind. There wasn't any difference really.

He was tired, but he'd phone Maxim to let him know about his meeting with the little old lady. Before he could make his own call, the phone rang.

"Mister Kennedy?" Her voice was breathless.

"Miss Turner, what can I do for you?"

She was to the point. "I need to see you, immediately."

"It's late. I only just got back."

"I've spoken to Teddy already and he said I should talk to you," she whispered urgently.

If there had been any possibility that he was not going to Sussex again, it was dispelled there and then. He breathed deeply and sighed before he answered.

"I'll be there as soon as I can."

"Thank-you, Mister Kennedy, Teddy and I appreciate it very much.

"Miss Turner, I thought you didn't have a phone."

"I don't young man. The garage does though."

Kennedy put the phone down and turned to see Beverley and Milly standing there.

"We're coming with you," Beverley said matter-of-factly.

"You can't, it's late and I don't know when I'll be back."

"All the more reason to come with you. Don't you think?" He didn't argue, there seemed little point. Beverley phoned Ray. They met them at Hammersmith, in a layby with little lighting. Ray was behind the wheel of the Lexus, with Eyeball and Ice. Lex was in the BMW with Big Lip. They all looked bulkier, there were things under their jackets which Kennedy knew were not lawful. He couldn't see an end to all this. It was bad enough that Beverley was in all of this, but Milly too? He never should have let them come. The little girl had fallen asleep by the time they'd closed the back door. She stretched out like only small children can. It was quiet on the road and they made good time. There was old time country and western playing on the radio.

Kennedy was not an expert. He couldn't tell how long Miss Turner had been dead. That she was dead, there was no doubt. She lay, broken and twisted amongst a pile of ashes and ceramic which had once been the resting place of her dear husband. A small trickle of blood seeped out of one her ears and from each nostril. She appeared to have hit her head on the side of the table when she fell. It was a shame that they hadn't gotten there quicker. Kennedy stood there for a few moments. Beverley was outside in the car, with Milly. Ray and the boys checked the rest of the cottage, but there was nothing. Kennedy leaned down and even though he knew there was little point, he took her pulse. Long gone. He didn't start barging around, he knew the forensic team would not appreciate it. It seemed she'd had a heart attack, but as he stood up, a horrible and disgusting thing dawned on him. What if someone killed her? Suppose the urn had been smashed first? Even though he wasn't a detective, the whole scene had the disgusting stench of murder about it. He bit his lip until he could taste blood. Things were going from worse to bloody awful. He heard a noise from the kitchen and he stepped back ready to fight or flee. Slowly, the three cats came out one by one. They at least had been spared the fate of their mistress.

Big Lip took a step back. "I hate fucking cats."

As soon as he got back, Kennedy phoned Maxim to tell him what had gone down. (He'd already called the boys in blue, but only once they were halfway home. The guns Ray and his men were packing were not good for public relations.)

"That is truly horrible," Maxim said with some understatement.

"What about the cats? Were they harmed?" Maxim asked.

"The cats are fine," Kennedy all but whispered.

He put the phone down and went to the window. It was snowing. Fine, fresh flakes of whiteness just like there had been in Manhattan. He cocked his head to one side and began to think. That was where he was standing when Beverley came back to join him after putting Milly to bed.

"Still a nobody?" he said without turning around. He

knew the answer, so he didn't know why he'd asked.

"Yes. She still thinks she's a nobody." Beverley put her arms around him from behind. He felt cold and distant. He was not an easy man to get close to. Every time she thought she'd finally gotten him to open up to her, it felt as though he was slipping away again. Nobody had told her how difficult it was to compete with a memory. Someone who could do no wrong anymore, someone who would always be golden. Beverley hated herself for being jealous of a dead person, yet that was how she felt. It would almost have been easier to have dealt with a mistress or at least someone who was physically there. She didn't know what to do. She knew that recent events hadn't helped, but in a way she thought that it would have brought them closer together, but instead they'd grown further apart. Her over-protective brother was not helping matters either. She'd been hoping for some decent sex, now this. Death was not an aphrodisiac.

She took her arms away from him. It felt as if he hardly noticed. She went back into the kitchen and watched the snow slide slowly down the window, she could feel tears welling up deep inside her. They didn't fall, they just lay there, not falling and not going away.

She felt rather than heard Kennedy come in behind her. "I'm going back to New York," he said softly.

The snow was falling heavily now. She nodded without turning around. She understood. The answers to all of this lay there. He had to go. She would not be going with him. She knew that too. She did not waste her breath by asking the obvious. He paused a few moments then went upstairs to check on Milly. She was fast asleep and had managed to knock all her teddies off the bed onto the floor. He picked them up and placed them carefully next to her, managing not to wake her. Gently, he kissed her on the head and went to pack. He would go to bed soon and sort out a flight in the morning. Both Beverley and

Kennedy knew that they would not be making love tonight. Shame, because it would probably have been the best thing for both of them. Beverley because she needed to be held and Kennedy because he was like most men, he made far more sense after he'd come.

He lay in bed aware of Beverley's back. Outside Big Lip and Eyeball kept watch on the house. Kennedy couldn't tear his thoughts away from the little old lady in the cottage. Why? What had she ever done to anyone? Forensics would have done their job by now. The police had not arrested Kennedy on suspicion, but did make it clear they might want to talk to him again at some point. Kennedy was refreshed with their down to earth attitude and capacity to be realistic. Very different than the do-or-die squad he'd met in Manhattan, with the exception of Lee. He was a paradox. Sleep did not come easily for Kennedy. The bent copper Caruso, O'Rourke, Ka-Lut, Lee and all the others blasted around his mind like an opera--a Peking opera. Kennedy was frightened, but excited as well. There was something about it all which made him feel alive. Obviously his repeated brushes with death had something to do with this.

And then there was Beverley. He felt so mixed up. She was a beautiful, sensitive woman who loved him dearly. He knew he would never find someone as good and loyal to him but he just couldn't let go of the memory of Debbie, no matter how hard he tried. And he resented having to. He didn't want to move on without her; why should he? He could feel himself getting resentful and angry about everything as Beverley lay next to him, her light nasal wheeze cutting the stillness of the night. The baby alarm, which Kennedy had kept installed in Milly's room was peaceful and quiet. He gazed at Beverley's back and the shadow of one her breasts and his resentment began to evaporate. Tension was bad for the skin, she would say. She was right.

25

The next morning he made some calls (he didn't tell Maxim he was returning to New York) and got the limit on his Mastercard increased. Beverley's goodbye was formal and still. Milly's was predictable.

"Don't forget Daddy, I'm nobody." She smiled and Kennedy tried to smile back. He was going to have to do something about this but he knew that he couldn't argue with the little mite and then leave.

The flight was with American Airlines and though he wasn't upgraded to first class, it was a very comfortable flight. His comfort soon ended, and if he thought he was going to hop into a taxi at JFK, he was mistaken. There were two of them— both big, both oriental. And they were swift. The door of the giant black Lincoln swept in front of them. The door swung open and Kennedy was bundled in. He was being kidnapped and no-one appeared to see anything. Even the man who hails the cabs was looking the other way. In New York, you tend to live longer that way. There was a strange smell in the car. Sandalwood. It mixed strangely with the bittersweet taste of fear in Kennedy's mouth. He was wedged between his two abductors. Could have been twins. Probably were. They were looking straight ahead and so was Kennedy as the limo wound its way through Queens.

A smiling face with kind eyes sat across from them. Face spoke. The voice was warm, reassuring even, and the eyes twinkled as he spoke. Still, Kennedy was terrified.

"Mister Kennedy,"

It got worse, Face knew his name. Several chins

wobbled in time with the motion of the car.

"...look around you, what do you see?" He motioned at the suburbs of New York passing them by, outside the darkened windows.

Kennedy tried to answer but had great difficulty. He couldn't help himself. His mouth was dry like he'd been pumped full of sawdust. Face saw his dilemma.

"How rude of me. I haven't offered you a drink. What would you like? Coffee, water? Maybe tea, after all you are English. A nice cup of tea?"

If Kennedy had anything resembling liquid in his system already he would have pissed his pants. He had never been in the presence of anyone who had such an evil persona yet looked like your favourite Chinese grandfather. Kennedy was about to answer but he was interrupted.

The eyes narrowed and the chins wobbled as he leaned forward and touched Kennedy on the knee.

"I recommend the water, myself. Coffee de-hydrates you and it seems to me you could do with some re-hydrating. As for the tea, it is not the same in the back of a car, even if it is a nice American one like this is."

Kennedy tried to be cool. He sounded like an idiot and he regretted it as soon as he said it. "Water, shaken not stirred."

Face motioned to one of his trolls, who leaned forward, opened the mini-bar, and poured some Highland Spring from a cold, unopened bottle.

"You don't look like James Bond, if you don't mind me saying so Mister Kennedy." He managed to make the Mister sound like an insult.

"I don't feel like him either," responded Kennedy. This did not sound either cool or clever and was far more appropriate and truthful than any other smartarse comment he could have made. He took the glass of water. There was even an ice and a slice. The troll could have carved himself another career as a barman. As he took a sip, the water seemed to stick in his throat. That he was about to die seemed to be the only thought shooting through his mind. Face was obviously a mind reader.

"Don't worry Mister Kennedy, we are not going to hurt you today." The overall statement sounded good but Kennedy was not feeling any better. He didn't know that one simple word like today could have such a vicious impact.

Face repeated his question as he waved his hand almost regally at the passing buildings. Traffic had forced them to slow down somewhat.

"What do you see?"

"I see people, buildings and airplanes in the sky." Kennedy felt like he was back in nursery school. He resisted the temptation to speak in a stupid voice like a four year old.

"Opportunity Mister Kennedy. That is what is out there. Opportunity and shall I tell you something else?"

"Please do." The sarcasm was lost on Face and his numerous chins.

"Dreams, Mister Kennedy. Without which you have nothing, just an empty shell of existence from one day to another. Nothing to hope for, nothing to build on, and no good thoughts to take to bed at night." He was quite the wordsman. Under different circumstances, Kennedy might have found himself listening because he wanted to rather than because he was forced to.

"Right, yeah I can see that." He took another sip of water. Two monsters sat either side of him, their knees digging into him like guys on the tube. Legs splayed. He wished he was on the tube now, as far away from here as possible.

"My people are Chinese." He stated the obvious.

"We are brokers, you might say, men who invest in the future. We deal in dreams and opportunity." He looked straight at Kennedy.

"My name is Wo-Kei. I am a business man from Vancouver. I help people come from my homeland in China to a better life in Canada and the United States. They come with their dreams and their hopes and I provide the means to see these dreams become reality." He was certainly telling Kennedy a lot.

"Business has been good. Everything was going well and then something terrible happens." They were on the edge of downtown Manhattan now and Wo-Kei nodded to one of the trolls who banged on the screen behind the driver. The car came gently and slowly to a halt, down a sidestreet. Kennedy stiffened, he dreaded that he was going to be killed and dumped like a piece of useless garbage for the dogs to sniff. His remains to be found by a bag lady.

"They take my daughter, my beautiful, sweet Ka-Lut." The face distorted and the chins did a macabre little dance against each other as he moved his head from one side to the other.

"I wasn't the cause of your misfortune." Kennedy felt as though he was on trial here and pleading his case seemed reasonable. After all he seemed to be in the presence of the judge, jury and executioner.

The face belonged to one of the most powerful and ruthless bosses of the Chinese underworld. Suddenly the eyes were like two piss holes in the snow and he was hissing rather than speaking. All human warmth had disappeared.

"But I may be the cause of yours. Unless you help me to get my daughter back." The words looped out like a piece of bad breath. Kennedy scratched his nose. Nervous reaction.

"How can I help? You're the ones who tried to kill me." He sounded a lot braver than he felt.

"You and your violin are mixed up in all this and it

wasn't I who tried to kill you. If it was, you would have been dead. It was the New York snakehead. The same ones who took my daughter."

"If you know who they are, can't you just get her back yourself?" He sounded a lot braver than he felt or for that matter appeared. His nose was getting itchier.

"They have stolen my dream, my future. I don't want to do anything which will put her at risk. They want a lever on my operations in Vancouver. They got jealous, thinking I was making more than them on my part of the operations."

"Were you?" It seemed a reasonable question, under the circumstances.

"I am a good business man." He waved both hands in the air. He looked like the friendly grandfather again. This man missed his calling in life, he should have been an actor. The gestures, the voice, the phrasing, the timing, he had the lot.

"I cannot do anything to endanger my little girl. Nothing. That is why you must do everything you can to find her."

"What can I do?"

"You wouldn't be back here if you didn't think you could do something. You lost something very precious and you want it back. It is the same for me. You have no choice."

"And if I don't help you?"

"Then I shall kill you."

He patted him on the knee in a gesture of sincerity. It was not needed. One of the trolls opened the door and helped Kennedy out. He found it difficult to stand for a moment as he had been wedged in for so long. It gave his demeanour a kind of comic look as he stood there on the sidewalk and wobbled a bit before he found his balance.

"I'll do what I can. I don't want you to have me killed." Talk about stating the obvious.

"We'll find you when we want you. You will be a very busy man." Wo-Kei looked straight ahead as he spoke then his head swivelled and he looked Kennedy straight in the eye.

"And Mister Kennedy, I did not say I would have you killed."

"Yes, you did." His reply sounded juvenile.

With Kennedy still fixed in his lizard eyed stare Wo-Kei made his final point.

"No. I said I would kill you."

The door of the limo slowly closed. The car and its unwelcome passengers headed for a duplex deep in Manhattan, leaving Kennedy standing there smelling his own body odour. He felt like he had just met the devil.

He looked down at his trousers. At first he thought he had pissed himself. They were damp and smelly and sticking to his crotch. Then he realised that it was sweat. He breathed deeply then started to walk down the alley back to the main street. With his crumpled and smelly clothes, Kennedy did not look out of place as he passed several homeless men and women, sitting on pieces of cardboard, with large cloths tied around their ears to keep out the biting cold.

"Howyadoin, buddy?" One of them said to Kennedy as he passed.

"Not very well, friend, not very well." He didn't even bother trying to avoid a puddle, though he'd seen it long before he stepped in it. The muddy tepid water splashed up his leg and inside his trouser, before dripping down onto his sock and inside his shoe.

26

He tidied himself up before hailing a cab, otherwise they wouldn't have stopped for him. A walk around New York, feeling the way he did was not high on the agenda. Manhattan was an electric place, guaranteed to make the most jaded of individuals feel like it was good to be alive. Today, however, he was feeling more than jaded. Even Manhattan could not work its magic on him. He needed to sleep and to work out what he was going to do next. The way things were going it was going to be a job just to stay alive. He'd done well so far. This trip was going to be a lot different from the last time he came, no swanky room at the Waldorf. His increased Mastercard limit was capable of withstanding some kind of assault but another stay at the Waldorf would have wiped it out with one hit. Even ordering a plate of sandwiches there would have maxed his limit. Your perspectives changes when it's you who's footing the bill.

He had the name of an economy hotel in the East Village. Some parts of the Village had improved over time but in this part you still did not want to let your guard down. Zero tolerance did not have quite the same impact here as it did in other parts of the city. The good mayor was still on the drawing board as far as this section of the neighbourhood was concerned.

He got in the cab and closed the door. A disembodied voice on a tape advised him to buckle up. It rather loudly though reasonably creatively, suggested that he do so to ensure that all drama was kept in the opera, where it belonged, as opposed to the road. The taxi driver didn't have a clue where he was going. That was par for the course. The tape machine might have had a better idea. Kennedy guided Ahmed the way you take a small child step by step through his first class. First the ABC then the joined-up writing. You know the score. Kennedy knew his name because it was on his license which was plastered all over the back seat. The automated voice cut in again, this time reminding Kennedy to get a receipt for his journey but this was hardly a trip which would be tax deductible.

Like something from a western, he limped into the foyer of the Manhattan Star hotel. It was certainly in Manhattan but star? Well, creative names have a way of suggesting rather than actually delivering. Kennedy thought his injured leg was getting better but it was hurting again. A throb which seemed to start in his calf and go all the way up to his groin. All he needed was a saddle and a pair of spurs and it would have felt like high noon. The man at the reception desk had an eyepatch. He would have found it funny but recent events had dried up most of his humour. The one eyed man smiled a toothless grin. Forget the western, all he needed was a parrot and he would have been at home on a pirate ship.

"Hello. I'd like a room please," Kennedy said. He put his bag on the floor. He dropped it the last few inches as he was hurting too much to bend down all the way.

"Sure, sir. Would you like the presidential suite or the one with the excelsior view." He smiled again and Kennedy realised that he was mistaken about the teeth. There was one, in the back of his mouth. Small dirty and probably rotten but certainly there in all its glory.

"What's the presidential suite?" Kennedy asked. He knew there was probably little chance of getting a serious answer.

"That's the room I'd give to the president should he ever come to stay." A small trickle of saliva seeped out of the side of his mouth.

"In what way is that different to the rooms you give anyone else?"

"Ain't no difference." The saliva was gone mainly because he'd turned and spat it into a bucket. He examined his handiwork before turning back to Kennedy.

"Right and the excelsior view?" Kennedy couldn't wait for the answer to this one. He was not to be disappointed.

"That's the view of the back alley. Only some of the rooms have it."

"How is that excelsior?"

"Some of our residents like to know there is another way out of the establishment." He smiled the one-toothed smile again. Kennedy could understand the sentiment.

"I'll take the one with the excelsior view."

"Certainly, sir." He handed Kennedy the key. "Room twelve, up the stairs, turn right at the top and its down the hall." Kennedy went to pick up the key. The man with the single tooth put his hand on top of Kennedy's. "That'll be sixty dollars a night."

"But I don't know how long I'll be staying."

"Pay each day then. Makes no difference to me."

Kennedy peeled off some dollars and deposited them on the desk.

"There's three days worth. If I stay longer I'll let you know."

"Fine by me." He picked the money up and made it disappear faster than a bigamist at a wedding reception.

Kennedy walked up the rickety old stairs with a lot more confidence than he actually felt. The room was everything he expected. The bed looked less inviting than the floor and the sheets suggested that once, maybe a long time ago when dinosaurs roamed the earth, there had been some colour in them. The pillow was identifiable only because it was near the scratched and broken headboard. Flat, thin, and yellow it resembled a small mammal just run over by an enormous truck. Something ran out of the tap in the corner. Chemical tests might prove that it was once water, but whatever route it took to the Manhattan Star had robbed it of any resemblance to something you drink. There was an unnecessary sign which read "not drinking water."

He threw his bag onto his bed and looked at the view. The alley stretched out below him for about twenty feet. A man was looking directly at him from a window which was touching distance away. He wasn't doing anything, just looking out of what appeared to be his bedroom window. He seemed to be harmless but Kennedy drew the single curtain which had been so painstakingly measured that it failed to fit the window properly. A masterpiece of design by any standards. Probably not done by one of the top designers in Manhattan but certainly by one of the most imaginative.

Kennedy didn't even bother looking for a phone. He locked the thin wooden door behind him. This was a hopeful gesture. If someone had wanted to get into his bedroom the lock wasn't going to make any difference. He left his bedroom to its fate and went back downstairs. The one tooth man was checking a book. He could have been looking to see if he had been awarded a Michelin star. He looked up and smiled. If he hadn't gotten the star, he was obviously going for it.

Kennedy made a gesture with his hand which was supposed to resemble a phone. One tooth nodded at a table with an old cloth on it, underneath pictures of what looked like Istanbul. He picked up the receiver and a voice answered straight away. It was one-tooth. Kennedy heard him in stereo as he was so near. In one ear down the receiver and in the other, for real. He was sure there was probably a better system but he was not in the hotel advisory game, so no point starting now.

Kennedy gave the number down the line and a yellow nicotine stained finger stabbed the digits out on the ancient switchboard. Pre-Casablanca. It did, however, give good service. Lee's voice was on the answerphone. Kennedy left the number of the hotel and his room number, although that was probably not necessary as the receptionist, owner, switch board operator, one-man-band would certainly remember his room number when Lee phoned back.

Kennedy nodded at the man as he put the receiver down. He'd obviously listened to every word Kennedy had said.

"I'll come and get you if he phones back, sir." He made the "sir" sound comical in the surroundings. But Kennedy could hardly complain about any of it since he was footing the bill and a return to the Waldorf was not an option.

He had only been lying on his bed for a few moments when there was a knock at the door. Room service. Lee was on the phone. That had been quick. Kennedy hurried down the stairs, he was feeling sorry for himself and was looking forward to talking to Lee.

"Kennedy, are you mad?" Lee had a point. Kennedy had expected him to raise it, only not so quickly.

"I had to come back, all the answers seem to lie here," he said glaring at the hotel manager who wasn't even pretending to mind his own business. He didn't have to listen in over the switchboard, he just had to sit there with a bottle of cheap Mexican beer and stick his nose in, where it wasn't wanted.

"Where are you?"

"The East Village."

He gave the name of the hotel which brought out a gasp from Lee. He described it in terms you wouldn't find in the good hotel guide and said he would be over as soon as he could. An hour at the most. Kennedy went back to his room and waited. The hour seemed to drag past.

Snakehead had power everywhere in New York, the East Village was no different. Lee didn't know it, but he was being followed by three men who did not have either Kennedy or Lee's best interests at heart. Lee parked his car and ran into the hotel unaware that his every move was being monitored. The three orientals sat well back in a sleek black Mercedes and watched Lee from a distance. Two in the front, one in the back. Their eyes looked as though they were connected to the same brain, moving as one and even blinking in time.

Lee knocked on room 12.

"Who is it?" Kennedy asked while opening the door. His precautions were getting a bit sloppy. Lee stood there smiling and blinking. Kennedy nearly hugged him but British reserve and Chinese decorum stood in the way. Lee came into the room and as Kennedy went to close the door, Lee stopped him.

"You're not seriously thinking of staying here, are you?" He looked around him in disgust.

"Who booked you in here?" he asked. Lee was sure that it was someone who hated Kennedy, there could be no other answer.

"My wallet. It's hardly bulging. I've given the man three nights in advance." He sighed. The room looked even worse now that Lee was here. On his own he was able to kid himself.

"Get your stuff. You can stay with me."

"Isn't that a bit dangerous for you?" Kennedy was becoming a master of the understatement.

"Not as risky as coming back here, that's for sure. Come on, I'm not parked far from here." He held the door open and Kennedy got his stuff. It didn't take long and they went downstairs, where he dumped the rusty key on the desk in front of the man with no dentist.

"I'm leaving. Any chance of my money back for the other nights I won't be staying?"

The world's worst hotelier smiled like a mongoose. "So sorry, your highness. The money has already been invested in future development for the premises. You're just a mite too late."

He sucked a piece of his remaining dinner off his tooth. He was enjoying himself. Kennedy had only been there a short while and the Brit had already got on his nerves more than any guest he could remember.

Lee grabbed Kennedy by the arm and steered him to the door by his elbow. "Come on, there's no point arguing."

"Sir," The man shouted after them. "I'm feeling generous, so I won't charge you for the use of the telephone." He shouted the word telephone as they were already out the door, but he knew they heard. He smiled, very pleased with himself and sat down in front of his ancient telly. He took a swig of the beer and picked his nose as he swallowed it. He would probably have not been so relaxed if he'd realised that Kennedy's leaving had saved his life. The snakehead would not have dealt kindly with the smelly manager of the Manhattan Star.

27

As Lee drove them away, Kennedy looked back at the hotel's broken neon sign. He knew that he would not be seeing that place again, unless he revisited it in a nightmare. They were both unaware of the Mercedes which swung effortlessly into the traffic, some distance behind them.

Lee had a secured parking area, not far from where he lived. Kennedy got out of the car and accidently stepped in some wet mud on the floor of the car park. "Shit!" he said. It summed up everything. Mud, shit, whatever—he seemed to be going through all of it and all at the time. He looked at Lee. At least he wasn't alone. He didn't know what he would have done without the help and support he was getting from Lee. A pang of guilt hit him as he thought of Beverley, then he banished it from his mind. Beverely was thousands of miles away and this was no time to be having these thoughts.

Hurriedly, they walked through the bustling throngs of people all talking, shouting, crying and screaming. There seemed to be food everywhere, all types and in all different stages of cooking. Glass fronted restaurants held unbelievable numbers of people, all trying to get attention at the same time. Their three trackers kept a respectful distance. They were not ready to show themselves just yet. They'd parked the Merc around a shady corner. There was no-one mad enough to interfere with it. They might as well have had a sign painted on the side of the car, announcing one step closer to death if you messed with it.

Lee had to make himself shout to be heard above the

noise of humanity.

"It's not far. We can get sorted then go and get something to eat. Alright?" He pushed past people in a way which was quite un- British but Kennedy did not protest. If they had done it his way they would have taken all night.

They came to a smart looking apartment block. Lee produced a key, almost like a magician. He seemed to have a quick slight of hand. He opened the door and they let themselves in. They walked along the corridor, turned the corner and Lee pressed the lift button for the third floor. Lee wasn't too keen on heights, so he'd always lived on the second or third floors.

Had they slowed down and looked back down the corridor they would have seen the three men catch the slow closing door just before it shut. With no doorman or closed circuit television, it was easy for them to slip in, like a slimy beast.

Lee opened the door of his apartment and let them both in. He removed his shoes and Kennedy did the same. The apartment was very tastefully decorated and Kennedy certainly preferred it to the Manhattan Star. It was small but neat, and had a very definite oriental flavour. There was wood on the floor as opposed to carpet, and as Kennedy followed Lee into the open plan front room he could see that the windows and skylight were designed in such a way to let in as much light as possible. "There's a lovely feel of space and room in here, even though it is small," observed Kennedy. He could not hide the admiration in his voice.

"Feng-shui. The space leading to your home or business should be kept clear of clutter and rubbish. It is supposed to be welcoming, like the open wings of the red phoenix." He smiled at Kennedy. There were very pretty etchings on the wall and an aquarium just to the side a few feet away from a small television and sound system. Lee put his bag in his room and pointed to the futon against the wall. Wooden, it was simple and elegant with a very inviting cover with little flowers all over it.

"You'll be sleeping there. Sorry I don't have a room you can have of your own, but this is Manhattan. Like a luxury yacht, you pay dollars for each metre." Kennedy didn't reply he was transfixed by the fish in the aquarium. Lee came up behind him and pointed to them the way a proud father would.

"They're very beautiful even though they're Japanese." They swum around with slightly more enthusiasm, almost as though they knew they were being watched.

"Japanese carp. If they weren't fish I wouldn't have them in here."

"Not keen on the Japanese?" Kennedy sat down on the futon. It beckoned sleep.

"No. Don't you know your history?" He looked a bit irritated, as he was blinking a bit more than usual.

"Yeah, but I thought... "

"You thought we were all the same," Lee interrupted.

"No, it was just I mean..." Kennedy felt awkward. Truth was he didn't really know what to say or do. He felt uncomfortable with the way this conversation was going. Lee was good to him and was being extremely co-operative. They hadn't discussed it but Kennedy knew that O'Rourke did not know he was back in New York and would be extremely pissed when he found out. Lee was not helping his promotion chances by helping Kennedy in any shape or form and he appreciated the risk he was taking.

Lee went into the kitchen which was just off the front room.

There was a small hatch through which Kennedy could see Lee washing his hands. Probably very wise, perhaps Kennedy was not the only thing Lee may have picked up in the filthy surroundings of the Manhattan Star.

"There's a big thing between the Japanese and Chinese. Always has been. The Japanese have always regarded the Chinese as the sick man of Asia. The Chinese have always hated being treated in that way." He was drying his hands and was clearly on a roll. It was a monologue which Kennedy suspected had been smoothly developed over the years and was built on a well-developed sense of smouldering resentment.

"Do you know that when Bruce Lee brought his films out and he was sticking it to the Japanese in his early work, people were cheering and clapping in the cinemas? That was what made him so popular; never mind his martial arts." He threw the towel back from where he had picked it up and came back through the door. He went over to the fish and had his back to Kennedy as he spoke.

"Of course I love my fish. They can't help the fact they're Japanese."

What he heard next brought a chill to the room and froze Kennedy to the spot.

28

"What's wrong with the sons of Nippon, my Chinese friend?" The words were spoken by one of the three men who were standing in the doorway leading to the hall. The one who spoke was standing in the middle. He appeared to be unarmed. The other two had semi-automatic pistols. One was pointing at Lee and the other was pointing at Kennedy. Neither had a silencer. That was a good sign. At least Kennedy hoped it was. If they were going to kill them here, they would have had silencers. If Lee was scared, he did not show it. One of the men gestured with his gun, for Lee to join Kennedy. He silently obeyed. He gestured again, and Lee sat down on the futon. Kennedy made a bit of room for him and they both waited for the three men to make the next move.

The one in the middle took a step forward, almost as if he was in a film and was finding a mark before he spoke his lines. He had a monocle and a Brooks Brothers suit under his coat. He was dressed like a member of the English gentry. He even had a small riding crop in one hand. His attire was that of an English gent but without a doubt he was a native of the land of the rising sun. "I am Japanese, Mister Lee, and I am as one with my fellow countrymen." He produced a gun of his own from under his rather smart coat. A nine millimetre. He screwed on a silencer. Both Lee and Kennedy took a deep breath. This was not looking good.

"Stand up, both of you!" he barked. His little specs rattled on his nose as he spoke. He looked comical and deadly at the same time, with his smooth coat and foul piece of death-dealing metal in his sticky paw. He licked his lips and ran his tongue around his teeth.

"You, both of you, have been irritating individuals." He certainly was Japanese. He couldn't pronounce the "r's". The were said like "v's." Again, another place, another time, it would have been funny.

Kennedy and Lee stood up, both breathing deeply. The other two men stepped apart. Kennedy got a good look at them. Both small, they were nasty looking pieces of work. One was completely bald and had little beads of sweat running down into his narrow, lifeless eyes. He had a jogging suit on. His name was Hung and he was fat. Many dead people had mistaken his corpulence for propensity towards slowness and an inability to move on his feet but he was an accomplished and enthusiastic killer. The snakehead often made use of his many skills.

The other was Khan. He was not so experienced a killer. Thinner than Hung, what he lacked in experience he made up for with enthusiasm and attention to detail. He was a warrior, not a farmer, and felt that making money by following the law of any land was for wimps. He despised nut gatherers. He was a meat eater. That was how he saw himself, and the world around him, through his one good eye. The other was there, but useless and dead. His unarmed fighting skills were not as good as Hung's, and many moons ago in a Shanghai bar, a fight with a Portuguese sailor had cost him. A flick of the wrist and a blade had severed his optic nerve. Quick, efficient and very painful. Often he would wake up screaming with the memory of it all.

The Japanese man spoke again. "We are going on a little journey. There are friends of mine who wish to speak to you."

"Wo-Kei?" Kennedy knew as soon as he spoke that he had made a mistake. The man looked startled and ruffled.

"What do you know of Wo-Kei?" He spat.

Kennedy didn't say a word. Lee looked at him with something in his eyes which told him to be quiet from now on in. The Japanese recovered his composure. Both Lee and Kennedy exchanged another look.

"No matter. We will find more out later. My name is Mishima. A truly great and imperial name," he said with some grandeur and pomp.

"Unlike you Mister Lee," he continued, "I love all things Japanese." He kept grinning, then spun towards the fish tank.

"However, I hate fucking fish!"

To emphasis this point he fired two bullets into the aquarium. Each one found their target and the remains of the two carp spiralled against the fractured glass as water spurted out onto the wooded floor, splashing Mishima's fancy suede brogues.

Suede? The whole scene seemed more and more bizarre to Kennedy.

Lee's body stiffened and he blinked several times. He looked really distressed and his adam's apple was bobbing about like nobody's business. Kennedy sensed that there was a lot more to this man and that he was unfolding before his eyes. Lee took a deep breath, swallowed, but said nothing.

The five of them took the stairs. As they left, Lee and Kennedy realised how the men had found Lee's apartment. There was a tell-tale smudge of dirt trailing from the lift to the Lee's door. It was mud, from the bottom of Kennedy's shoe.

They each got into the leather bound interior of the Mercedes.

29

Khan was driving. He had more confidence in his one eye than he had in Mishima or Hung's two. It was his car and he wasn't going to have anyone else drive it, especially a Japanese. The snakehead were happy to do business with anyone if the dollar was right but it didn't mean the ones in the lower orders like Khan or Hung had to like it. They certainly had to live and work with it though.

There was a lot going on in the organisation and they had never been busier. They, like everyone else up and down the ranks, knew about the kidnapping of Wo-Kei's daughter, Ka-Lut. They knew that she had been snatched in order to put pressure on the old man from Vancouver. They also knew from the grapevine that it was working. He'd been taken by surprise, like so many of them.

Shang, the boss in New York, had always worked in harmony with Wo-Kei in Vancouver. The soldiers brought the immigrants into British Columbia by land or air, ripping up their false passports before they arrived in New York claiming refugee status. That got them into America. They would cross the border through the Indian reservations where the guards in their four-by-fours couldn't go. It would have started a political war if they had been found crawling all over the burial grounds of the ancients. The snakehead were happy to take the risk of being discovered by a few Indians. They were never a match for the gangsters and a horde of hungry immigrants thirsting for a new life in the city of bulging wallets. Of course, what Khan and the others knew was that there was no good life. The immigrants were only worth money to the snakehead if they couldn't afford to pay the balance due upon arrival in New York. That was it, that was the whole point. They were put to work in the sweatshops and restaurants of Chinatown in order to pay what they owed. Naturally, ridiculous rates of interest meant they would never pay it off. They would just work and work.

Everyone, except the immigrants were happy. They were just swallowed up in the forty block area of Chinatown under a blanket of over one hundred and fifty thousand people. That was just the official figure, the true one was much larger and besides all the Chinese just looked the same to the Americans. The presence of the Koreans just served to complicate matters. Snakehead liked complications, which didn't actually involve them. It usually meant they made money and everyone else connected to the foul organisation made money. Top banana, thought Khan as he drove them through New York.

They had passed City Hall and were heading for Foley Square. Khan watched his speed in the powerful car. The New York traffic cops were sharp and vigilant when it came to speeding. It would be very bad for business to be caught out tonight. They had important people in the car. Little Dragon had taken a personal interest in them and had ordered that they be taken, unharmed tonight. That was the key to everything. The stealing of the violin and the kidnapping were linked, if only by timing and by the fact that the New York snakehead were responsible for both. Everything had kicked off when Shang had been disposed of and the Little Dragon took control of the empire.

No-one, but no-one knew the identity of the Little Dragon except close associates and since no-one seemed to know who they were, for the time being the identity and the whereabouts of the Little Dragon remained a mystery. Little Dragon was the one who said Wo-Kei was getting too big a cut for simply passing immigrants through. Little Dragon wanted to destroy Wo-Kei and to take over his substantial interests and powerful links to China and organised crime. If everything was sorted out properly the snakehead would be the most influential crime syndicate in North America. They were already on their way. Dollars equalled power. The more you had of one, then the more you had of the other.

Shang had been a very respected boss and the way in which he was so quickly taken out was a big fright to everyone in New York who thought their position was unassailable. They found a piece of him floating in the East River. The rumours flowed as thick as the filthy slime in the water. Some said that what they found was still in a trouser-leg, but nothing else, others said his head was stuck on a stick at some point on the shore between the Brooklyn and Manhattan bridges. Whatever the score, he was double-crossed and taken out. No-one could have gotten to him without the support and co-operation of Pai-Lan, the hitman with the double knives. He was the one rumoured to be responsible for actually dealing Shang the death number. Just the kind of thing he would have done, with pleasure and artistry.

Khan drove past the county courthouse then a few minutes later he was driving up Park Street, at the bottom of Columbus Park. He slowed down and a huge corrugated door opened as if by magic and he eased the Mercedes into the open driveway. Light pierced the night then was suddenly cut off as the superpowered doors slammed shut very fast. Any following vehicle would have been cut in half, had they been foolish enough to attempt entry.

The place was very busy, this was one of the nerve centres of snakehead. Operations and administration for the immigration smuggling all took place here. Many dollars in the right place meant that at this stage, interference from authorities was unlikely, though there were many in the American justice system who could not be corrupted. In these instances, threats to their families were often more effective. But all that business was tiresome, when what the snakehead really wanted to do was to make serious money. The computer age had helped. All they needed was a few minutes notice and in a flash everything disappeared as though they had never been there.

Lee and Kennedy did as they were told and got out of the Merc. Their three abductors did the same and they stood there for a few moments before a large metal door opened. There was a kind of smoky effect which made it quite difficult to see what was going on and where everyone was. Two large rotweilers were held snarling and spitting by two Chinamen who looked singularly ill-suited for the task. Their combined body weights must have been less than that of the hellhounds. But Lee and Kennedy's attention was not fixed on the dogs, their eyes were fixed on the chair. Wooden and simple, it was a very specific type of chair. The correctional institutions used them to electrocute people. Tied in it and with a metal cap on her head was a very young, pretty Chinese girl. Tears and blood streaked her face. There was a large electrical cable running from the chair to a generator by the side.

As if by magic and almost as though he was entering from stage left, Pai-Lan appeared. "That's Dog One" he said as he walked towards Lee and Kennedy. He gestured to one of the slavering hounds. "And that's Dog Two." He pointed at the other one, straining at the leash as though it knew it was being talked about. "Number one and two. Life is all about numbers, gentlemen." Pai-Lan held his hands out in a welcoming gesture, which could not have been more inappropriate under the circumstances. The light was dim but reflected just enough of his hands to show the two dancing, flying birds near his wrists. If there was any doubt in Kennedy's mind that he was face to face with the man who had tried to kill him, it was eradicated by the flash of holster under each armpit. Each held the wicked, vicious instruments of death, one tipped with deadly nightshade—his hellish trademark.

"Welcome, my friends. Relax, you will not be harmed tonight. I have brought you here because it is time to talk." Kennedy's death can wait. He snapped his fingers and a table and three chairs materialised as though by magic. Lee and Kennedy sat down, not because they were demonstrating a willingness to partake of Pai-Lan's hospitality, but due to the force of Khan and Mishima's strong hands on their shoulders. Pai-Lan licked his lips, sat down, and started to whistle the tune to Mastermind. Lee tensed. For a few moments Pai-Lan whistled on happily, then stopped. He addressed Mishima, Khan and Hung directly.

"The Little Dragon thanks you for your work tonight. You have done well."

All three tried to look suitably grateful for this message of thanks from someone they had never met before, but feared more than death itself.

"I don't like the Western style of bullshit, so I will come straight to the point. We have Ka-Lut. As you can see she does not have a very long life expectancy."

Pai-Lan leered at the terrified girl in the chair, with her torn blouse and tattered little tartan skirt. A small trickle of blood was visible under one eye. "Power surges are notorious in this part of Manhattan. Isn't that right my Japanese friend?" He directed his question to Mishima who, proud that Pai-Lan had addressed him directly beamed as he answered back. "Happens all the time, Sifu."

The last words saw Lee stiffen a bit, which Kennedy

noticed. He didn't know what a Sifu was but it had an effect on Lee. His eyes went back to the pitiful sight of the young, defenceless Ka-Lut, strapped into the death chair and he could feel the bile rising from deep within his stomach. Then he looked at Pai-Lan and knew that before tonight he had never known the taste of true hatred. It was rich, spicy, foul and sour and it was all in his mouth and deep in his gut. If he could have, he knew with absolute certainty, he would have killed Pai-Lan with his bare hands there and then. Pai-Lan knew it too. It appeared to give him deep satisfying pleasure.

"I know you have been seen by Wo-Kei. That is the only reason you are still alive. That and the fact I failed to kill you the last times our paths crossed." He smiled and Kennedy knew he was facing the very personification of evil. "The two of you will go tonight and you will tell Wo-Kei what you have seen and you will give him a message. He snapped his fingers and a piece of elaborate paper was brought over. It had Chinese writing on it. Pai-Lan grunted and bent the paper in a complicated series of folds, the birds on his hands dancing as he did so. He handed it to Kennedy who reluctantly took it.

"What about her?" Kennedy pointed at Ka-Lut. Pai-Lan sniffed.

"I've already had her. Tight, she bled a bit but that's how I like them." He smiled at Lee who simply blinked back.

"Why did you kill the old lady? What had she ever done?" Kennedy had been waiting to ask that question. Pai-Lan allowed his head to drop to one side and he looked almost adolescent.

"Me? Not me. I can assure you." He smiled which robbed him of any resemblance to an innocent young man.

"You..." Kennedy didn't get the rest out as Pai-Lan interrupted him. "You! You are in no position to speak about anything. Now go and understand one thing, the next time we meet you will know that you were only ever one thing."

"What's that?" Kennedy said with more bravado than he actually felt.

"A dead man without a box."

He sneered as the large steel door opened and the rotweilers barked, almost on cue as Lee and Kennedy were ushered out into the freezing cold night. Kennedy had one more question.

"Why the violin?"

"The Little Dragon appreciates fine music," Pai-Lan shouted.

The power door shut just as the last image of the lonely petrified little girl seared itself into Kennedy's mind's eye. He dropped to the pavement, speechless, his body racked with tension. Lee helped him back up and stood there, biting his bottom lip.

"What do we do?"

"There's nothing we can do, except wait for Wo-Kei to make contact. He still held the piece of paper in his hand.

"What does it say?"

Kennedy narrowed his eyes against the biting wind. Lee opened it and paraphrased it. "What I expected. Wo-Kei is to get out of the business altogether and to sign it all over to the Little Dragon. If he does so his daughter walks if not she...well you saw her in there." He folded the paper up carefully, attempting to hide the fact it had been read already. No point in making matters worse by showing disrespect.

"Can't we just get your guys and storm the place?" Kennedy knew it sounded a bit too much like Batman and Robin to be a serious consideration. Lee smiled but there was no warmth in it.

"They'd be long gone, and their fancy lawyers would sort it and there would be an unexpected power surge. It wouldn't help anyone."

"What about you? Surely not calling in with all this will affect your badge," Kennedy said. This made a lot more sense than his previous statement about storming the fortress.

"Yeah." Lee looked thoughtful. "You've got a point. It means I wouldn't be at the precinct anymore and have the piss taken by O'Rourke. Now there's a pleasant thought." He arched his eyebrows.

"Piss taken. That's an English term. You're picking up bad habits from me," Kennedy said. Then a sudden thought came to him. "Sifu. What does that word mean?"

Lee licked his lips. "Why?"

"When he said it, I saw you react as though you knew what it meant."

"It doesn't matter just now. It's a Chinese thing." He breathed out heavily and looked at Kennedy.

"Anyway. Come on. Let's get home and give my fish a decent burial," he said this with no humour and absolutely no trace of a smile. They hailed a taxi which at first wasn't keen to take them. They did look somewhat dodgy, there had been little chance to freshen up when the three men had come calling. Lee had money in the apartment but none in hand. He gave the driver his rather nice watch as collateral until he could get into his place and get cash. The driver looked like he would have preferred the watch, particularly as both of his own wrists were bare.

30

Kennedy waited in the freezing cold. He felt like shit and pondered the events of the last days. The stolen violin and related events hadn't gotten much press coverage in England. After all, Posh Spice had got a parking ticket and Cherie Blair had chipped a nail. The Brits got their priorities right when it came to what they wanted to read in the newspapers. Or were they told what they should expect to read in the newspapers; he wasn't sure.

He hugged himself and bounced up and down to keep warm. The light came on in Lee's apartment. He was taking a while. Kennedy wondered what was up, if anything. His mind wandered back to the newspapers in England and their obsession with all things pointless and trivial. George Best trips up on a paving stone and there is a front page devoted to it, with a picture of a council worker on the front; the very man who may have been responsible for not seeing to the offending stone in the first place. Then there would be a series of articles about whether or not it was actually George's fault in the first place. It wasn't the fault of the people who were famous, it was the people who ran the papers and the individuals who mindlessly bought them without trying to influence what actually went in them.

The broadsheets weren't much better. They would have the same story about the parking ticket or the paving stone then carry stuff about the statistical averages of such events. They would wheel out the Professor of Stonemasonry from some University, which used to be a

Polytechnic, who would spout about the case for the usual fee. He laughed to himself. Despite all that he missed England and its abundance of something which the Americans seemed to be lacking, irony. There was something refreshing about cynicism and sardonic takes on life, if they were kept in check of course.

On the other hand the Americans were great for their enthusiasm and optimism. They always made you feel that anything was possible. If you worked in a greasy burger bar, then you had the feeling that one day you might own it. Everyone who worked with you had the same outlook. There seemed to be pride in how things were served and the customer actually mattered. Kennedy smiled as he cast his thoughts back to the good old UK. There, if you went into a fishmonger and asked for some fish, you would get a strange look from behind the counter. Then the man would say, "What do you think I am, a fishmonger? Look if I give you fish, everyone will be coming in here asking for it and then where would I be? An exaggeration perhaps, but there was definitely that kind of feeling afoot in the not so United Kingdom. He slapped his hands against his body again. It looked as though the taxi driver (who remained nameless for Kennedy, as he could not read the scruffy i.d. on the back of the seat) was going to take off with Lee's watch after all if he didn't hurry back with the cash.

Just in time a breathless Lee was back with the required dollars. He threw a few extra in, just for good measure. After all, the man had been waiting a while. There was no point in waiting for him to draw Lee's attention to the fact that he could have been off delivering a celebrity to some up-town address. The watch, somewhat reluctantly, was handed back with some ceremony. As it passed out of the window to be retrieved by Lee, a streetlight flashed and Kennedy glimpsed some writing on the back. An inscription of some type. He hadn't been able to make out what it was.

"Sorry I was so long, I had to make a telephone call."

"Girlfriend?" Kennedy was trying to be light-hearted. He had not heard mention about a woman in Lee's life and he was definitely not gay. Kennedy came from the rather optimistic school of thought which was that all men could tell if members of their sex were gay or not. Not a view which was universally subscribed to, but a popular one nevertheless.

"What does it say?" Kennedy asked, gesturing at the watch.

"A quarter after midnight," Lee said after checking his watch and walking towards the apartment building. He waited for a car to pass before crossing the road.

"No, I didn't mean that," Kennedy said as he crossed some way behind him. His knee, shoulder and leg were all hurting. In fact, his whole body was hurting. He felt like one giant sore, emotionally and physically.

"What did you mean?" Lee asked as he buzzed the apartment of his next door neighbour.

He had not brought the keys with him when they had been taken against their will. When he'd come out the second time he'd forgotten to bring them again. The stress of everything was beginning to take its toll on him. The neighbour said something in Chinese, which translated into something like, "that's twice you've rung my bell. How many times are you going to do this? I'm tired and want to get some sleep." Lee apologised in Chinese and the neighbour relented and buzzed them in. For good reason, Lee had not told the little old man about the visit from the snakehead. That was not something which would have inspired confidence in the apartment block. In fact, Lee would probably have found his tenancy permanently revoked.

Lee pulled the door open and walked towards the lift, still with his back to Kennedy.

"I meant what was written on the back of the watch?"

He felt that this was not a conversation which Lee was trying to encourage. It seemed more like he would rather have been talking about something else.

"Oh, that. Nothing really," he said almost absent-mindedly. The lift appeared with a reassuring whirr. He went in first. Kennedy slotted in behind him. It was not a big lift. The three unwanted visitors had obviously used the stairs because there was no way they could have got in the lift together.

"Looked like something to me." Kennedy's tone was actually more to the point than he had meant it to be.

"Well, it was nothing. Alright?" His eyes narrowed and told Kennedy to drop it; he did.

They walked into the apartment. The water from the fish tank had made a right old mess. One of the carcasses of the fish was lodged in the broken glass. The other was on the floor looking lonely, sad, and pathetic. Kennedy felt a lump in his throat as Lee bent down. He stroked it gently then picked it up and went into the kitchen. His feet made a scrunching noise as he walked over the gravel which had spilled out onto the wooden floor. He pulled a piece of kitchen towel off the roller on the wall and carefully and respectfully wrapped the fish in it. Kennedy did not react when Lee whispered a few quiet words over the fish's carcass then went through to the toilet. The tell-tale sound of flushing made it clear to Kennedy that the fish was now enjoying all the delights of Manhattan's sewer system. Lee did not hold a service of remembrance in the toilet. Instead, he came out drying his hands, with a relaxed look on his face.

"Are you alright?" Kennedy asked.

"No, I'm not alright. But you have to move on from one moment to the next, from one day to the next, and so on." He smiled at Kennedy.

"But then you understand that, don't you?"

This caught Kennedy off-guard. He hadn't expected it. He sucked a tooth before answering and sounded less than convincing. "Yeah, I think so. I mean yes, you're right. You can't hold onto the past all the time, really." He did not look very comfortable.

Lee nodded. "There's a lot of bad things gone off recently. They all suck but you can't keep dwelling on them. You seem to be caught in the past all the time."

He came forward and put his hand on Kennedy's knee. Another time, another place under different circumstances, and Kennedy would have told him to get lost.

"Murray," Kennedy wasn't sure but he thought that was the first time Lee had used his Christian name, "...why won't you let go?" Kennedy did not insult his intelligence by pretending he didn't know what he was talking about. He looked distant and thought for a little while before answering.

"I can't help it. Every time I think I'm moving on my thoughts go back to that night in London." His eyes misted over as the memory came back to him. He ran his tongue over his teeth as though tasting the bitterness of that eventful night.

"I lost a wife, and my daughter lost a mother," he said as he stood up and walked over to the window and looked out at the street. There was no-one who appeared to be watching the apartment. Anyway, they were both past caring.

"Don't throw the two together. You're just thinking of yourself. It's all about you, not your daughter. Your loss."

Kennedy turned round as though he'd been set on fire. Lee's words cut him like a freshly honed carving knife. "How dare you! What do you know about it anyway?"

"I know it, because I've done it. I've been there. Believe me. I didn't stop feeling sorry for myself until someone told me to stop pretending my grief was for others, it was for myself. It had to stop. You have to live for others Kennedy, otherwise you may as well head straight for the graveyard now and get in the box." He did not mince his words.

"What happened?" Kennedy could feel his anger subsiding.

"Everything in good time, but mark my words, stop feeling sorry for yourself. You'll just keep losing more and more."

"Wise words."

The reply was not Kennedy's, neither was it Lee's. It had come from Wo-Kei. Uninvited guests were becoming a bit of a habit. Lee blinked, then walked slowly back to the centre of the room. He looked like a prize fighter claiming the middle of the ring. Wo- Kei was flanked by the large men who Kennedy recognised as the trolls from his last encounter. They looked exactly the same as before but Wo-Kei looked different. There was something missing. He just looked less menacing. He looked more like what he was, a tired old man who just wanted his precious daughter back in the loving bosom of her family.

"Don't you have any locks on this apartment?" Kennedy asked, never taking his eyes off Wo-Kei.

"The kind of people who have been coming would not have been stopped by locks, Murray." He used his first name for the second time that night.

The trolls stepped aside a bit as Wo-Kei came forward. They had to, it was a small apartment and there wasn't much room.

"You have a nice place. Mister Lee." Wo-Kei's observation was completely ill-placed not to mention unwelcome. He had not come to rent or buy.

"The entrance is nice. Resembles the open wings of a red phoenix," Kennedy said trying not to sound like a funny man. He would have succeeded were it not for the fact that his voice went up a few decibels at the end of his sentence.

Wo-Kei looked at Kennedy. "I am familiar with such concepts, Mister Kennedy." Something had definitely changed. He was almost being polite.

"I have something for you," Lee said. He stood still. He had no desire to go the way of his fish so harshly dealt with earlier that evening.

Wo-Kei nodded and Lee walked very slowly over to where he had left the piece of paper. He turned and handed it to Wo-Kei who sat down, uninvited, on the ornate lacquer chair. His brow furrowed as he read. The trolls stood, troll-like either side of him as he digested Little Dragon's message. He looked even more shrunken than when he had first come into Lee's apartment. He sighed and put the paper down on the table in front of him as though it was a piece of diseased flesh.

"They will be getting back in touch with you. Tell them I'll do whatever they want. I want only my beloved back, that is all." He stood up. Kennedy couldn't believe that this broken old man was the same maniac he'd met earlier. Was there nothing love couldn't change? He clearly wanted his daughter so much, he was prepared to walk away from his criminal empire.

"They will tell you what and when I think," Lee said accurately. Wo-Kei nodded and stood up. The trolls had more presence now and looked infinitely more frightening. They were probably planning to fax their c.v's to the Little Dragon, as their boss appeared to be preparing to abdicate his throne. Kennedy couldn't help but admire the smoothness of the operation. It was a master stroke of genius by the Little Dragon, whoever he was. Wo-Kei was going to walk away without a fight. Incredible. He couldn't even storm their fortress. Ka-Lut would have been fried to a crisp, in seconds. No-one alive could have got the drop on these people. They appeared to hold all the cards.

He walked out of the room, followed by the two minders. They heard a sneeze as the door closed behind them. The stress of the situation already seemed to be affecting Wo-Kei's immune system.

Lee watched from the window as the two bruisers helped their now vulnerable charge into the back of the car Mercedes were the only car of choice for these gangsters, regardless of which city they operated in. Pull over every Merc in the city and you would catch them. Had it not been for the teflon principle, the police would have done just that. It's one thing getting hold of them, it's quite another making anything stick.

"I've had enough for one night. Let's get some sleep. I don't think anyone else will be bothering us tonight," Lee said as he turned away from the window. The Mercedes accelerated up the street; a couple of vendors jumped for their lives.

Early morning sunlight glistened through the window despite the fact that it was the middle of winter. Lee woke Kennedy with some herbal tea.

"I remember you like this stuff. There's more in there." He pointed to a little ornate teapot which stood on the kitchen top, like a sentinel for all things good for your body.

"When we're ready we can go down to the precinct and face O'Rourke. It's time he knew about this," Lee said.

"He'd go mad if it was kept from him any longer," Kennedy said as he took a sip of his tea.

"He'll go mad anyway," Lee said as he walked through to the bathroom, his flip-flops beating a rhythm against the now clean and tidy floor.

"Lee," Kennedy said just before he went into the bathroom.

"Yeah, what?" His right flip-flop completed the beat as he came to a stop.

"Last night. That word sifu. What does it specifically

mean to you?" Kennedy said.

"We'll come to it when it's ready. Everything comes in its own good time. Your English, you should know that."

"I've got Chinese ancestors," Kennedy said, drinking some more of the delicious tea.

"Then show it," Lee said.

"Sorry?" Kennedy was puzzled.

"Start showing more patience. That's the Chinese way." He beat one more pattern out with his flip-flops as he went into the bathroom and closed the door. Kennedy went up to the pot to get some more of the tea. He wasn't sure what it was but he guessed there was some ginger in there somewhere.

31

O'Rourke was furious. His face contorted like a fish under water. He slammed the desk with his fist as he shouted at the top of his voice at Lee. Kennedy wasn't spared the wrath but it was being targeted at Lee, who sat there motionless, displaying almost no emotion. He'd told O'Rourke everything and Lee, in turn had been called moron and some other stuff which Kennedy couldn't quite make out. In his temper, O'Rourke, an Irish American, almost sounded Scottish. Eventually it looked like he was finished. Nothing could have prepared him for what happened next.

Two smart looking men strode into the precinct house. Both tall, very short haircuts. High and tight. They marched straight up to the desk, flashed a couple of pieces of plastic, and then burst into O'Rourke's office. The desk sergeant sat speechless, his mouth open wider than the New Jersey turnpike. The two men stood with authority: black shoes shining like they'd been buffed by a laser, grey slacks with creases which could open letters, white shirts, plain blue ties, and navy blue blazers. They held their small identity cards out in front of them.

"What the fuck!" O'Rourke was to the point.

"FBI, that's the fuck," one of them said.

"The operation monitoring the activities of the organised criminal within the Chinese community is what brings us here." His card told everyone that he was agent Corleone. The other agent carried a card with the name of Brady on it. He didn't speak and stood stock still.

O'Rourke was speechless, and sat down in his chair.

In a machine gun manner, Corleone continued. "Senior agent Lee has been in charge of the on-going operation which has been taking place from this precinct. As things are hotting up, as you might say, we have come to join the proceedings, at our superior's request. They both acknowledged Lee.

"Good morning, sir."

O'Rourke nodded back and stood up. For O'Rourke it was anything but a good morning.

"Why wasn't I told about this?" he asked through clenched teeth.

It was Lee who spoke. All deference had left his voice. "Too tricky. Think Caruso. We thought there might be others."

This was too much for O'Rourke.

"You mean me?" He threw the words out like a javelin.

Brady spoke for the first time. His voice was surprisingly quiet but sharp like an ice pick. Everything about him was precision.

"No-one was suggesting that," he said.

"Well?" O'Rourke turned on Lee.

"Well Sir," Corleone reminded him. O'Rourke eyes bulged out of his head like a landcrab on coke. He spluttered something completely unintelligible and stormed out of the room, throwing himself past Corleone and Brady.

"It's okay," Lee said to the two agents and partly to Kennedy who was still transfixed with amazement. Even Lee's body language had altered. Something else had taken place, but Kennedy couldn't quite put his finger on it.

"He'll be okay, when he calms down in a while. He's embarrassed at the way he treated me. He would never have done it if he'd known. He's a good cop." Lee walked over to the window. He looked like he owned the room now.

"The man's an asshole," Brady observed. Corleone nodded like an academic putting his weight behind a fellow professor's thesis.

"Maybe, but he's still a good cop."

O'Rourke came back into the room. He looked like he'd considered his position, thought about his pension, and come to the only possible conclusion. He had to stomach this completely or walk. He had no choice, even though it hurt like hell.

"Welcome back, Mister O'Rourke. We were just discussing the matter in hand; please join us."

Lee took a seat at the table in front of O'Rourke's desk. He gestured for O'Rourke to sit at his own desk. O'Rourke seemed grateful.

"What were you saying?" he asked.

"We were just agreeing that you are both an asshole and a fine officer," Lee said with a smile.

O'Rourke sat down with a thump. Considering the rough time he'd given Lee, he had to admit he was actually getting off lightly. He had to take it.

"I see," he said and arched both eyebrows.

"I must say that I was very pleased that you had not gone the same path as Caruso. That would have been a great shame and a waste of a long and distinguished career," Lee said.

It was taking Kennedy some time to get used to the clear and authoritative way in which the new Lee spoke and acted.

Lee looked at Kennedy. "If you don't mind, I'd like you to wait outside while I brief the others and bring them up to date. There's nothing you don't know and I'm sure someone will find you a cup of herbal tea."

Kennedy stood up like a schoolboy who had been asked to leave the headmaster's study. He opened the door put himself on the other side and then shut it quietly behind him. Officer Wallace was still there, open-mouthed. When she saw Kennedy she smiled.

"Some tea?"

"Yes please," Kennedy said but with less of the schoolboy demeanour.

He waited a short while, then Officer Wallace came back with his tea. She smiled as she handed it to him.

"Thanks."

"That's a cute accent you've got there," she said with a smile. She was not flirting. Officer Wallace did not flirt. You got that wrong at your peril. There were a few in the past who had misunderstood. They rarely left with anything other than the correct impression. She was just friendly. That was her nature. Kennedy smiled back and was about to say something when the noise of O'Rourke's office door opening took his attention. Just as well, he was about to say how pretty she was. A big mistake. Kennedy had enough on his plate without messing up with Officer Wallace.

O'Rourke came out of his office followed by Corleone, Brady, then Lee. All three were smiling but O'Rourke's was forced and looked like it had been painted on. They shook hands almost as a gesture of goodwill. O'Rourke looked like he was touching an icicle when he took Lee's hand. He was still in a state of shock. After all, Lee had kept his cover up for two years and it would take a while for things to sink in. As Lee turned to walk toward Kennedy, something seemed to occur to O'Rourke.

Brady and Corleone went in search of coffee. They looked hopefully at Officer Wallace who looked them straight in the eye. "You may be the bureau but neither of you have got a fancy accent like him." She pointed at Kennedy. "So you can get your own." She then pointed at the coffee machine which needed filling up as well. She smiled and resumed her paperwork. They looked startled for a moment then shrugged their shoulders and went over to the machine and started to grapple with its complicated instructions. It would take a while.

"Sir?" O'Rourke spoke to Lee's back. Lee turned.

"Yes. "

"How did you manage, if you don't mind me saying, to appear to be such an idiot for such a long time. No-one had a clue."

"That was easy Officer. You treated me like one. Couldn't have done it without your help." He smiled and turned back to Kennedy.

O'Rourke looked like he had inherited that nervous blink from Lee. He disappeared into the sanctuary of his office. At last he was on his own and he could lick his wounds properly. There was a bottle of whisky in the cabinet which could benefit from some attention.

"There's not much for you to do here now. It's probably safer if you return to England. I've arranged for the bureau to meet your expenses, to ease things a bit for you," Lee said.

Officer Wallace was busy instructing the two agents how to fill the coffee machine. They had failed the test.

"Thanks, I appreciate that."

Kennedy was still having difficulty adjusting to the new Lee, who carried an air of authority about him. Word had spread like wildfire around the precinct house as policemen were looking at Lee in a way they had not done before. All of them were racking their brains trying to remember if they had jumped on O'Rourke's bandwagon and caused Lee any distress. They obviously didn't know the man so they had no way of knowing whether or not he was the vindictive type. They were also judging him by their own standards. They would have been going for the jugular in his position. He had not had a good time of it.

"Why did you come here like this?" Kennedy asked.

"There was corruption going on. But we weren't sure to what degree. Recently the main troubles have all come from the snakehead and it was felt that I was the right man for the job."

Kennedy listened intently. "Do you think the violin will ever reappear?" he asked.

"Possibly. Let's face it, they won't have cut it up for scrap."

Kennedy winced.

"I'll sort a car out for you. You can stay at my place tonight, then we'll have you on the plane tomorrow." He snapped his fingers at an officer at the desk who came rushing over.

"Arrange a car for Mister Kennedy, please."

"Certainly, sir."

"Oh, one thing." Lee held his wrist up.

"The watch. It was something I got when I graduated from the Academy. He undid the strap. The inscription read, "to the best from the best." Kennedy nodded in understanding.

The air outside was still below freezing when Kennedy came out of the precinct house and got into the back of the squad car. It was about to pull off when someone slapped the roof hard. Kennedy pressed the button and the window came down with a whirr. It was O'Rourke.

"What happened in there?"

"Don't take it too hard," Kennedy said to O'Rourke who was leaning against the car.

"Are you laughing at me?" he said quietly.

"No-one's laughing. You were just doing your job, but..."

"But, what?"

Kennedy swallowed before he spoke. "You could be a bit kinder to people. It wouldn't hurt you know."

"But then everyone thinks you're soft."

"You want to try soft sometime. It's not so bad, you know."

Kennedy gestured to the driver who slowly pulled away. O'Rourke stood there for a few moments, then went inside to attend to his whisky bottle.

The driver seemed keen to make conversation. Kennedy wasn't. When they arrived at Lee's apartment Kennedy let himself in and tidied up a bit. It was the least he could do. A few hours later, the phone rang. It was Lee. He'd arranged for Kennedy to be on a flight home tomorrow. Kennedy had something at the back of his mind but he couldn't quite get a hold of it. It was only when he'd put the phone down that it came back to him. Sifu. What had that meant? Lee was going to tell him. He mumbled the word to himself as he went into the kitchen to make himself a cup of tea. It was all coming to an end with just a few loose ends to tidy up. Murray was relieved and starting to relax a little. Then his cellular rang. The voice on the end of the line was hard, simple and clear.

"They've got Beverley and..." Ray paused before finishing the sentence. The bile had already begun to rise in Kennedy's throat when he heard the dreaded last words. "...your daughter."

32

They'd come in and out with no sign of a struggle. Big Lip and Eyeball had been wide awake outside Kennedy's house. They saw nothing and heard less. He was not about to lose anyone else precious to him. His flight home was a blur, but to his surprise Lee had checked in and was seated next to him. Ray was at Heathrow like he said he would be, with Lex and Ice in the short term car park of Terminal 3, Level 2. They all got out of the car when they saw Kennedy and Lee come out of the lift. Ice had parked the car in that section so they could see without having to leave the Lexus. They were a sober looking bunch. No Rolexes, diamonds or designer gear. When there was a rumble afoot that stuff always got left behind.

"Who's he?" Ray didn't look at Lee nor did he express any pleasantries to Kennedy.

"Lee. He's F.B..." Kennedy didn't get any further.

"You've brought a yank fed. Are you fucking mad?" Ray took a step forward.

"Don't worry. We'll do everything your way. I've got a bad memory and terrible eyesight." It was Lee who spoke. His eyes were narrow and focused.

Ray looked him up and down. "Alright. But don't forget this is my manor." Lee nodded but looked slightly puzzled.

"Manor?" he said quietly to Kennedy as they walked to the Lexus.

"I don't know how to explain it."

"Don't matter," Lee said. This was obviously not something which was going to be solved with a badge and reading someone their rights.

They got into the car whilst Ice went to the machine and paid for the ticket. He was swearing when he returned.

"Three quid. We've hardly been here anytime." He eased himself into the driving seat as Ray spoke.

"They've made contact."

"What did they say?" Murray heard his voice but it could have been anyone speaking. He had not slept a wink since hearing the news of Beverley and Milly.

"They want you."

"Let's give them me."

Ray sighed as though he were talking to someone who had difficulty grasping simple concepts.

"Who do you think we're dealing with here? They'll cut you into little pieces and we'll never see you or your..."

"Alright, alright. I get the message." He put his head in his hands. He didn't want to hear the rest, his imagination could fill in the gaps.

"We're going to give them something else." Ray said quietly, as he slipped a Wailers CD into the system. Kennedy looked up. He didn't like the look on Ray's face, which he could see reflected in the wing mirror as they sped along the motorway.

"Pull off here." They were the first words Ray or anyone else had said in the twenty minutes or so since they'd left Heathrow. Ice indicated and took the slip road off which curved back under the motorway. He drove into the entrance of an old and obviously disused industrial estate. It was like a scene from the old Avengers series with shutters blowing in the wind. High above them wide-bodied aircraft flew in and out of Heathrow at more than one a minute. Ice pulled up next to a medium sized warehouse close to a series of weed filled ditches.

"What now?" Kennedy didn't recognise his own voice. It was hard, raspy and cold. The hatred in his heart, for the people holding Beverley and Milly had poisoned his vocal chords.

"Now, we wait."

"What for?"

"It'll take a while, but someone will let me know where they're being held."

"How can you be so sure?"

"This is London. Nothing I can't find out, with the right favours or the right money."

"What if they've taken them North?"

Ray turned round to look at Kennedy and Lee. "You better pray they haven't—are you the praying kind?"

"I am now," Kennedy said slowly.

They sat there for several hours till the call came. When it did the sound of Ray's mobile cut through the silence like an old-fashioned cut throat. As Ray flipped the top open with one hand and put the phone to his ear, the BMW with Eyeball and Big Lip in it, pulled up next to them. Ray was a man of few words.

"That was Rat." Ray turned to Ice who nodded.

"They've holed up near New Cross," he continued as Ice turned the engine on and headed the car south of the river, following Ray's whispered instructions. Ray always whispered before a rumble. Just a habit. Eyeball and Big Lip followed closely behind. There were thunderclouds high in the dark sky. It took the best part of two hours to get across London. Kennedy felt as though he was going to throw up every inch of the way.

They pulled up in a dark secluded lane. The clouds had done their job and a strong rain was falling. The windscreen of the Lexus was a sheet of water cleared every few seconds by the wipers, which were set on the delay option. Some distance off in the shadows there was an outline of a large building. There were no windows. Ray got out of the car and went to the boot of the BMW. He opened it to reveal a small arsenal. He selected an Uzi and stepped aside as Eyeball and the others helped themselves to a variety of machine guns and semi-automatic pistols.

"How are we going in, Ray?" Lex spoke quietly but quickly, thanks to the adrenaline pumping through his system. It was also not a time for noise.

"Through the door, and Lex..."

"Yeah?"

"You only shoot the ones with guns."

Lex was about to protest, then he remembered a scene way back when and he stayed silent. Ray had a point. Trigger happy was an accusation Lex had to take on the chin. At least the victim had been a tow-rag, no use to society, or was it victims? Lex couldn't be sure it was all so long ago.

Ray whistled and they started to move off.

"Hey!" It was Lee who was still in the back of the car.

"What?" Ray had little patience in his voice.

"What about me?"

Kennedy was relieved he did not say us, he didn't have the stomach for this.

"Stay where you are. The less you see, the better. That way you don't have to forget so much."

Lee nodded and put his head back inside the car. There wasn't much he could say to that. Kennedy bit his lip as he thought about Beverley and Milly. The men moved quietly through the undergrowth. Ray had been right. There were no lookouts as the kidnappers did not expect any visitors. After a few heartbeats they were at the double doors of the old barn. Like the wild west, Ray kicked the door open and rolled through the opening closely followed by the others. Lee and Kennedy saw the flashes of gun shots before they heard the lethal popping sound of automatic gunfire.

It was only a few minutes, but it seemed like an age before Ray knocked on the window of the car. Kennedy opened the door.

"It's over, you can go in."

Kennedy walked through the dark guided by the light coming through the open door. There were four of them. All Chinese and all dead. Three looked like they were asleep except for small traces of blood. The fourth one had half of his head missing. Kennedy didn't need to ask where the dead man's brains were. The soft spongy mess under his feet answered that one. Over in the corner, an ashen-faced Beverley was holding Milly who had her eyes closed and was not moving. Kennedy half fell towards them. Beverley's tone was quiet but cold. It was the shock.

"She's alright. She's been asleep through all of this. It was her way of coping." Kennedy reached out and touched Beverley's cheek. She knew what he was thinking.

"I'm alright. The Chinese don't check for black women." She gave him a small half-smile.

Lee walked deeper into the barn. He was following the sound of humming, like a swarm of bees. Only they weren't bees, they were human. About forty Chinese men, the latest cargo to be smuggled in. They stood there, in their own shit and piss, unblinking and looking straight ahead at Lee. There was to be no golden future for them. He turned away. Kennedy was already carrying little Milly back to the warmth of the Lexus.

On the way back Ray called the police. He knew they wouldn't be pushing themselves on the forensics. Four dead Chinese gangsters. Good result all round, really.

33

It was a few days before things seemed to go back to normal. Lee had gone back to New York having seen little and remembered nothing. It was best that way. Milly did not appear to be suffering any obvious trauma. But things were not so rosy between Kennedy and Beverley. Kennedy got in bed beside Beverley. He felt like making love and reached out for her. She groaned and moved away from him, then turned and allowed him to hold her.

"How have you been?" she whispered in his ear.

"It's been all go," he whispered back. He tried to caress her but she moved away again. "No," she said firmly.

"What's wrong?" Kennedy felt hurt and rejected.

"Nothing. I just don't feel like it," she lied. Everything was wrong with them but she didn't feel like going into it there and then. There was a time and a place. She knew that everything that had happened recently was not your everyday, normal, run-of- the mill events. But he hadn't come into the barn for her. It had been Ray. She had every sympathy for him, but she just didn't feel she was getting what she deserved out of the relationship. She'd done some thinking and she knew that there was no point thinking if you weren't prepared to speak. Everything in its good time. She allowed him to cuddle her again but he knew not to try to take it any further. She'd made that much clear.

He lay there for a while but was restless. He went downstairs and put the kettle on. For some reason he made himself a cup of coffee. First he'd had in a long time. Must be the first Englishman who comes back from New

York and fancies a rest from tea. He kicked yesterday's copy of the Evening Standard. It was still wrapped in plastic and lay on the kitchen floor. The paper boy knew to deliver it to the back door. Beverley obviously hadn't noticed it or hadn't bothered to pick it up. The most likely explanation was the first, she was too tidy to just have left it there.

He put his coffee down on the table. It was too hot to drink. The steam rose to the ceiling past the picture of him which Milly had drawn at her nursery. Great circles of crayon just went round and round with a couple of blobs in the middle which were suppose to be eyes, he thought. The time to worry was if he went to the nursery to pick her up and someone recognised him from Milly's picture. Then he knew he was looking bad.

The plastic came away from the paper with a satisfying rip. It was one of the nicest things to come back to. English newspapers, even if it was the Evening Standard. It was English and most of all it was about London.

The front page was like a vision of hell for him. The headline screamed out at him, "Snakehead Kidnap". He sat down slowly at the breakfast bar and read the story which came with the headline. It first explained that there had been a news blackout on the trial proceedings because so many people were at risk. Nineteen Chinese men and women were on remand awaiting trial. The people had been tracked and brought to justice by members of Scotland Yard's Organised Crime Group. The story got worse. Kennedy thought it had only really poisoned North America. He had not realised that Europe was so infested. The piece told the story of one hostage being so terrified he had jumped from a 20 foot high window and escaped barefoot. The operation in Britain had been called Kronos and had been on the trail of the most kidnappings Britain had ever seen. Many of the hostages had been held in South East London and it was all connected to the smuggling of illegal immigrants. They came through Dover in specially converted trucks. Many of the Triad's operations originated in other parts of Europe like France and Italy. The piece then told the story of the shoot-out. Ray was right. They made it sound like a battle between the gangsters themselves. No mention of anything or anyone else. It was like none of them had ever existed.

He knew that he would be getting Lee up from his bed, but he phoned anyway. A sleepy voice on the other end of the phone, in New York, told him that he was correct.

"Lee, it's Kennedy."

"Don't tell me that you're back in New York," he grunted.

"No, it's about what was in yesterday's paper. It was waiting for me, on my kitchen floor."

"The triad involvement in England?" He yawned.

Kennedy was slightly disappointed. He hadn't expected him to know about it. "Yeah, that's right."

"It came over on the teleprinter. I was going to phone you." Lee yawned again, which irritated Kennedy but it was very late back in New York.

"Well, sorry to bother you."

Kennedy suddenly felt a bit stupid. He wasn't a policeman, why was he carrying on like one? After saying goodbye to Lee, he put the phone down and went back to bed. Beverley was fast asleep. He did not make the mistake of trying to get her interested in making love again. He'd gotten the message the last time. He lay there for a while trying to get to sleep then he sat bolt upright in bed. Something had hit him like a thunderbolt. His eyes were open and alert as though he'd been plugged in to the wall socket. He knew exactly what he had to do next.

34

Wo-Kei felt his power draining from him like the water after a rice harvest. He had worked so hard and so long to build his empire. Money and all it could buy were things which he had worked for ever since he could remember. Powerful men had other people do things for them. Men of consequence answered to nobody. You did the telling, others did the doing. He'd realised this when he was very young, probably still suckling at his mother's breast. He'd made up his mind long ago that he would be a man of consequence, an individual who would have others answer to him.

When he'd first gone to Canada, he was already a gangster. But things had gradually developed through the years. He'd already been immensely rich and very powerful. A real Triad bossman. Canada had opened up new horizons to him. He'd quickly realised that what he'd had before in terms of power and money was chickenfeed. As he became more influential in the organised activities of the people smugglers, he started to feel more powerful than any national politician or businessman. In many ways he was. He cared for nothing except money and power. That was until his only child, his beautiful daughter Ka-Lut was born to him and his wife.

He'd had many mistresses but it was his wife who had given him the child who would carry his blood on and into the future. She had become the most important thing in the world to him, even more precious than his business. Private schools and privilege which only serious money could buy opened up whole new worlds for her. At twenty, she was very young but extremely astute, and despite his best efforts she knew everything about his business and how he'd had acquired it. Her new beginning at the music school in New York should have heralded happy times for Ka-Lut, Wo-Kei and his family. Instead, the stupid bodyguards had allowed themselves to be caught off guard and she had been snatched from under their very noses. One had been killed in the kidnap operation. The other had survived to be able to tell Wo-Kei all he needed to know which was everything he didn't want to accept. He hadn't wanted to hear about how his precious angel of innocence was in the hands of scum he was used to controlling. Now because he cared for nothing else except getting her back in one piece and alive, he was preparing to step down from his operations and hand over power to the Little Dragon.

No-one knew Little Dragon's identity, that was the power of the new don to be. Complete and utter shadow. Wo-Kei would have bet his life that with his web of power he could have revealed Little Dragon. But no. He'd known from the start why they had kidnapped her. He'd also known that the longer his powerlessness appeared to be connected to his lack of information about Little Dragon, the more his influence was shrinking amongst the triads.

But Wo-Kei had developed this whole scheme—using men to appear wealthy and powerful as a result of their new life in the United States and Canada, then devising the overland route. First they would come into British Columbia. Then to gain access to the United States they would go to a native reserve, southwest of Montreal. This had become known as Smugglers' Alley. Others would be smuggled across Lake Ontario, all to end up in New York. There they would swell the coffers of Wo-Kei and his associates by millions, every single day.

The European end of operations was equally lucrative. Not as big, but growing, particularly with the chaos developing in Europe. Borders were crumbling and immigration control was succumbing to political interference by misguided governments wishing to be popular. The result was an ineffective barrier to organised crime across Europe. The same things had been developed in North America. Good for the triad, good for business and exceptionally good for Wo-Kei.

That was then, this was now. He knew that if he did as he was told he would get Ka-Lut back alive. He'd made up his mind to take her and the rest of his family as far away as possible from the empire he had built. It was no longer going to be his anyway. Little Dragon would inherit the lot. Little Dragon would clearly be more powerful than Wo-kei, and there would be little incentive to let people know the true identity. The fear and power lay with not knowing. Maybe that was the problem, people had gotten to know him too well Wo-kei mused as his private Lear jet screamed through the air at 40,000 feet on its way to Fuzian.

He was going to officially hand over the reins of power. Only by doing this would Little Dragon know he was serious and thus ensure the life of Ka-Lut. Big Man and the others would only swear allegiance to Little Dragon if Wo-kei came in person and announced his plans to step down, face-to-face in Fuzian.

The jet would land on a small airstrip (little more than a piece of tarmac) in the middle of the wilderness south of Shanghai and north of Jinmen. The authorities did not pay attention to it so long as the triad kept within the boundaries of unspoken rules. Strange, but they would only have trouble if they created it. It was as though organised crime was part of the function. If there was no organised crime then you would have disorganised crime. A kind of Yin and Yang effect.

Wo-Kei did not want to step down. If he'd been able to he would have killed Little Dragon with his bare hands.

There was still a part of him which thought that maybe some time, in the future, an opportunity would arise for him to taste revenge for the loss of his empire. For some, the humiliation was the hardest part to bear. He had to come and admit defeat having been taken out by an enemy, whom no-one knew.

The landing lights were on as the jet completed its final approach. The global positioning system told the pilot that he was spot-on. He did his final checks and respectfully announced over the tannoy that Wo-Kei and his travelling companions should buckle up. The pilot was careful to keep the tone respectful. He was in the employ of the triad so he knew that this was one of the last journeys Wo-Kei would make as a don. But Wo-Kei did not get to where he was by being anything other than a homicidal maniac and this was not a time to push or forget manners. Wo-Kei about to lose everything, and for a girl child. The pilot lowered the undercarriage and kept the nose in line with the lights running up the middle of the runway. He could understand if Wo-Kei's only child was a a man- child, then it would all make sense— but a girl? He shook his head as the wheels hit the runway with a bump. He lowered the nose wheel which came down as the anti-skid system cut in. There was some rain on the runway and no-one, least of all the pilot, wanted to end up anywhere except safely at the end of the strip. He applied the reversers and brought the plane to a surprisingly gentle halt. He and his co-pilot put on their hats and were at the door to bid farewell to Wo-Kei and his three associates. Wo- Kei was due to fly back to Vancouver later the following morning. But in the dangerous and unpredictable waters of triad politics, no-one could be sure of anything.

Wo-Kei bowed his head as he exited the jet. He looked smaller, weaker to the captain than he'd ever seen him before. He looked shrunken and ill. His face was sallow and his chins looked even more numerous and looser than ever. His heart was clearly strained to breaking point. The next day or so was not going to be kind to him. It was common knowledge that after this trip it was straight back to New York via Vancouver to meet the Little Dragon or his representative and take charge of what was left of his daughter, having handed the power leash over.

Wo-Kei squinted through the slight curtain of rain. Any other time he would have had an umbrella to protect him from the wet. His expensive clothes were not worn with getting wet in mind. But tonight he was past caring. Big Man was waiting in the back of a huge custom built Mercedes at the edge of the runway. The driver held the door open but he seemed less deferential than usual. It was as though everyone knew what was happening. Wo-Kei got in the back of the car as the plane was already being refuelled. He was about to experience the evaporation of his power first-hand. Big Man nodded to Wo-Kei as he sat next to him.

"Where is the car for my associates? Wo-Kei asked.

Big Man sniffed. "I had word from Little Dragon. I have been asked to make this as quick as possible." His tone softened a little as he said the next words. "It is all over for you. Wo-Kei. Even if you got Ka-Lut back and managed to dispose of Little Dragon, the loss of face is something from which you will never recover."

Wo-Kei nodded. His associates stood in the driving rain, a further insult which Wo-Kei could do nothing about.

"You have the papers?"

Big Man looked at the briefcase in Wo- Kei's hand. Wo-Kei nodded. All the documents necessary for transferring the control of the operation to Big Man was there. The Little Dragon had stipulated that Big Man was to get his own boys into Vancouver and take over the operation. It was a master stroke. By doing this, Little Dragon made sure that there was no possibility of Wo-Kei staging a last minute rally. Big Man, in a matter of seconds already had more power and was guaranteed more money than he ever had when Wo-Kei was in charge of the North American side of the operation. There was nothing else to do. The lights of Shanghai twinkled in the North as Wo-Kei handed the briefcase over.

"Thank-you," Big man sniffed. And for the first time he bowed his head in a slight gesture of deference and respect. They both knew it was an empty and pointless thing to do. Wo-Kei hated him for doing that.

Wo-Kei sighed and got out of the car. He said nothing but slammed the door shut. His three travelling companions were now truly soaked. Big Man said something to the driver and the massive beast of a German car silently disappeared. Wo-Kei said nothing, just turned and walked back to the plane. He appeared to stumble and one of his men reached out to help him. He angrily pushed him away and carried on walking that strange and shrunken shuffle back to the waiting aircraft steps.

Wo-Kei did not say a single word as the plane finished its refuelling. Nor did he speak for the entire flight back to Vancouver. He remained silent after further refuelling and throughout the flight back to New York. He was a shadow of his once proud former self.

35

Maxim was whistling to himself as he tidied things up in his workshop. Everything was going well with the various instruments due to be dispatched to grateful maestros and orchestra all over the world. Of course they were not the only clients. There was the spoilt brat in Geneva, who could hardly play a note. Her father had arranged for a very special viola to be at her disposal for four weeks, along with the very best tuition money could buy. Pointless, the child was moderate at best, not worth spending serious money on. Masters and maestros were born not created. There was a magic, a very special something which could not be artificially injected. So few understood that but Maxim did. His whole life had been dedicated to matching up masters with instruments that could take them to a higher level. And he knew when a pairing was right. Millions of dollars changed hands in the hope that something, some spark, would leave the instrument and enter the player.

He bit his lower lip as he prepared the acid he used to clean some older pieces of pipework and metal. It was his own recipe and he was always careful to wear gloves when he handled it. It hissed as he added more ingredients. He liked that, it sounded like his very own orchestra tuning up. That was something he would have liked to have had, his own orchestra. But he'd never been rich enough. He'd always been the broker for the rich men and their toys but not enough of it had filtered into his own pockets. It had been a source of growing resentment in him. Others got rich, he just made money.

But now, because of his recent activities and careful planning, all that was about to change. He bit his lip again. He was very excited. He put the large bowl of acid by the piano and went back to tidying up his work area.

"You're a busy man, Maxim," Kennedy said as he stepped out of the shadows. He'd let himself into the studio. All the time he'd spent coming here meant that he knew a trick or two about where Maxim kept his keys and which doors led to where. Maxim dropped the piece of flute piping he was about to treat. He picked it up, but his hands were shaking.

"What-what are you doing here?" he asked, completely taken aback. Kennedy was standing by the side of the piano. He nodded at the gloves on Maxim's hands.

"Tidying up some loose ends, are you?" He spoke softly and with an assured air unfamiliar to Maxim. He licked his lips and slowly put the piece of piping down.

"There's always work to be done, you know that," he said. He could hear the sound of his own heart pumping. It was even louder than the generator which provided the electricity for the workshop. He breathed out quietly. Kennedy's next words felt as though someone had stuck a red hot skewer through his bowels.

"Why did you do it?" Kennedy drummed his fingers on top of the piano.

"Why did I do what?" Maxim said. But he knew exactly what Kennedy was getting at.

"Cut it out, Maxim. They couldn't have gotten the violin without a tip-off. That was you. Why?" Kennedy had raised his voice and his face was now red and angry. Kennedy had told himself he wouldn't do this, but he couldn't help himself. Maxim puffed his chest out. He almost resembled a politician on the campaign trail.

"It was nothing. Simple. You had the violin. I had the insurance. The Chinese take the instrument. I get the money." He made it all sound so reasonable.

"Miss Turner didn't know that you'd insured it, did she?"

"No, of course not, that wouldn't have made sense. She wasn't supposed to have found that out."

Maxim was making less and less sense. With each passing minute he was beginning to resemble a trapped rat.

"Where did I come in this?"

"You weren't supposed to get hurt," Maxim said. He was not convincing.

"By that you mean I was supposed to die at the airport?"

"No, they had their own ways. I mean I don't know." He was sweating profusely now. Kennedy was looking calmer.

"You hooked up with them, because they were doing more and more of their filthy work through Paris, weren't they?" Kennedy moved his shoulder. He had a nerve in his shoulder which was giving him a twinge.

Maxim nodded.

"And the old lady. I was supposed to get wrapped up in her murder. Why did you kill her?"

"He didn't, it was me." The pain in Kennedy's shoulder was gone now. It had moved to another part of his body. It had more than a little to do with the cold tensile steel of a pistol barrel pushed deep into the side of his neck. It belonged to Raoul. He was smiling. His moustache was longer than Kennedy remembered but this was not the time to remark on that.

"The silly old bitch did me a favour. I didn't have to finish the job. She checked out when I smashed up that old jar. She was getting nosy. You would have been there had I gotten there earlier, but I was late. Bloody English traffic."

"How did you know?" Maxim asked Kennedy. He sounded a bit more relaxed now that Raoul had joined the proceedings.

Kennedy did not find it easy to speak. The barrel was deep into the side of his jaw. That was, however, much better than having the contents of the gun in his jaw.

"The cats," Kennedy managed to get out through gritted teeth.

"What do you mean?" Raoul pushed the barrel deeper. It was hurting in the most serious style.

"Maxim said he'd never met the old lady. Then he asked me about the cats. It didn't add up. It just took a while for the franc to drop."

Kennedy felt as though the barrel was going to come up through his tongue. He remembered what Lee had said about patience. Raoul was pushing so hard now that his body weight was forward over his toes. Kennedy could feel that Raoul was beginning to squeeze the trigger. The sequence was obvious. Bullet left gun, entered head, end of Kennedy. He did not fancy that. He pushed his jaw hard against the barrel, then suddenly relaxed and thrust his right hand up pushing the gun away. As Raoul fell forward, Paris's finest dibbles rushed in. As agreed with Kennedy, they waited until they heard a confession before interfering. Kennedy had not been foolish enough to try anything alone, he wouldn't have left the workshop alive if he had.

The police were quick, smooth and everywhere. They were fast enough to stop Maxim slipping to the floor in a mass of fleshy self-pity, his shirt front already soaked from tears of frustration and regret. The gendarme however, were not quick enough to stop Raoul from falling onto the bucket of Maxim's acid. There was serious damage done to his hand as skin peeled away from flesh like an over-ripe fruit. Some had gotten onto his moustache which was already hanging off his face. The whole effect gave him a kind of crazy under done look.

The police dragged a screaming Raoul out of the

workshop to administer first aid. A half walking, half hopping Maxim was marched out close behind him. He'd lost his trousers in the process and his lower belly was hanging over his underpants as he finally gave up the struggle to walk and was dragged to the waiting police van. Kennedy could not be sure but it sounded as though the Frenchman was laughing and crying at the same time. There could be no doubt about the screams still coming from Raoul as the police tried their best to administer to his wounds. The sound was like that of a rabid dog in its final death throes. There was at least some small justice for the little old lady in the simple Sussex cottage.

36

"All the pieces seem to be fitting together," Lee said slowly over the phone. He was on the other side of the Atlantic, but he sounded as though he was in the next door neighbour's bathroom.

Kennedy waved at Milly as she played in the garden with Beverley.

"Yeah, it seems that way. I'm booked with Virgin," said Kennedy. He was looking forward to seeing Lee.

"Good, give me the details and I'll meet you at the airport."

From the garden Beverley looked over at Kennedy then turned quickly away as he caught her gaze. She'd already made up her mind about what she was going to do. She was seeing Cordelia later and wanted to keep Milly with her. They wouldn't be going to the airport. She looked back at the window, Kennedy was gone.

The jets screamed into reverse and the red and white 747, lurched down the runway. Kennedy felt a surge of adrenaline. He was rapidly falling in love with this city. He was thrilled by the outline of Manhattan as the pilot banked his plane high over the Empire State Building. He thought about Milly. She was young enough to make the adjustment to another life. Who knows, maybe that would be a good idea. He was feeling very relaxed. Virgin had upgraded him. At last. He though it was never going to happen. The big seats and the attention to detail had made the whole flight very relaxing. He felt as though he had just had a massage on the upper deck. Even the twinge in his shoulder was not there for now.

Lee was waiting in Arrivals. They hugged. It seemed the appropriate thing to do after all they'd been through. Lee could sense the feeling in Kennedy as they drove through Manhattan.

"You really like it here, don't you? " Lee had got that right.

"Yeah, if only you could get the crime rate down." He smiled.

"We're trying you know. It's all these Chinese who make it so difficult, you should know that." Lee laughed and turned off the freeway. The laughter left him quicker than the customers of a restaurant with a health scare. The car which had been following them closed right up behind them, the one in front slowed right down and the unlikely sandwich slowed to a crawl.

Two familiar figures, complete with guns, had their doors open before the cavalcade had even stopped.

"Don't resist," Lee said. Kennedy needed no further advice as Mishima and Hung helped them from Lee's car. Khan was driving the one in front. Kennedy couldn't see who was in the car behind. He couldn't get his neck turned that far around. The twinge in his shoulder came back as they were bundled into the obligatory Mercedes.

"The Little Dragon wants to see you both," Mishima said. The tone in his voice suggested that this was something which was supposed to impress Lee and Kennedy. It did, but the emotion was fear.

Massive rainclouds loomed, suspended in the sky like messengers of doom. And once the doors closed behind them, they were driven to a building in downtown Manhattan.

Inside the large empty building, it was as though night had already fallen. There was a chair behind a table and a large sofa off to the side. A huge single arc light lit up the scenario like a school nativity play. Mishima, Khan and Hung stood back by the door. Kennedy and Lee knew, without looking, that at least two guns were trained on each of their backs. The table, chair and sofa were nothing out of the ordinary. What held their attention was the fact that each had an occupant. Kennedy's mouth was dry and his throat was rasping. Evil hung heavy in the damp cold air. A shaking, sweating form was on the sofa. One side of his body was already limp, and the other was shaking where he lay. He was not recognisable at first, but after getting used to the light, Kennedy and Lee realised they were looking at Wo-Kei.

The other two were instantly recognisable. Pai-Lan was leaning against the table, grinning like a snake and Ka-Lut was sitting on the chair. There was no emotion in her face, but neither was there blood. She was dressed, head to toe, in black designer gear. A kidnap victim, she was not.

It was Ka-Lut who spoke first. She looked straight ahead.

"Strokes are such unfortunate things." She smiled and then slowly turned her head to look at the dribbling, twitching, Wo- Kei. She turned back to Lee and Kennedy and then stood up.

"Some of our people are coming to look after him." She smiled then looked back at Wo-Kei again.

"Of course, they may be too late. You can never tell with these things. If he makes it, there is a rest home somewhere for him." She looked back at Kennedy and Lee and walked towards them and stopped. She blinked a few times and the grin was now clearly deranged.

"He made me as him. I was taught by the teacher. You target what you want then you strike without hesitation. Nothing, but nothing can be allowed to stand in your way." She walked back to the supine form of her father.

"The shock was too much for him when he realised his precious daughter was the engineer of his downfall. I had tried to break it to him gently, but he took it very badly, as you can see." She smiled that evil little smile as she stood over her father and stroked his face. The conqueror over the vanquished.

Lee said very quietly but still loud enough for everyone to hear.

"Little Dragon."

She bowed without taking her eyes off either of them.

"Since you are about to die, I have indulged myself and decided to meet you both for one last time."

Ka-Lut focused on Lee.

"Mister Lee, you are very special. Why do you waste it on the fat-bellied yankees. Join us. A new start and a very special beginning awaits you, if you show sense."

Lee stepped forward a few paces. Pai-Lan looked thoughtful and stroked his lower jaw. Wo-Kei had checked out of this world and looked like he'd been accepted into another. A small trickle of saliva dribbled out of the corner of his mouth. The fluid stained the front of his expensive blue and green club silk tie.

"Show sense. You mean like the people on the Happy Dancer?" He stood with his legs apart. If he was scared, like Kennedy, he wasn't showing it. Little Dragon was puzzled and looked at Pai-Lan who had stood up from where he had been resting against the table. He cocked his head to one side and did not take his eyes off Lee, as he spoke to Ka-Lut.

"It was nothing much. One of the grain boats we lost in a storm. Big money cargo but we made it up on the next one." He opened his coat, the two knives were clearly visible under his arms. He also started whistling his favourite tune to himself. It was barely audible above the hum of the arc light. He ran his teeth over his tongue.

"Nothing much!" Lee screamed and took a few steps forward. Mishima and Khan leapt out of the shadows but stopped dead at a gesture from Ka-Lut. Pai-Lan was looking very interested now.

"You scum, you dung eating scum." The veins on Lee's neck were standing out, proud, throbbing and pulsing with blood. He looked like he was going to explode with anger.

"My brother was on that boat." He spat it out like a piece of poisonous venom. The dawn of understanding began to spread across Pai-Lan's face.

"The brother. He was a sailor, he wasn't in the hold?" He opened his coat fully exposing the blades under his arms. Lee nodded in response to Pai-Lan's question. Ka-Lut looked irritated. She was not used to being in the dark about what was going on, but she was about to be enlightened.

"And there was another brother, wasn't there?" Pai-Lan was looking very pleased with himself. This was better than Mastermind. Lee nodded again.

"His name was Tei-Yon, wasn't it?" Lee nodded for a third time. The veins on his neck stood out even more. Kennedy thought he could actually see the blood pumping through them.

"What?" This time it was Ka-Lut who spoke.

"Tei-Yon was a peasant. Shot his mouth off. I sorted him out. He bled like a pig and died like one." He threw his head back, enjoying the memory. Light danced off his shiny, hairless head.

"His wife was pregnant!" Lee cried through clenched teeth as he slowly moved towards Pai-Lan.

Ka-Lut smiled as she spoke. "Looks like you've got some unfinished business. Master Pai-Lan."

He drew his mouth back away from his teeth and gave a rictus like grin. "I've started so I'll finish. Prepare to die like your pig brother, Lee. Maybe you will be the first to die with a cry." He stepped forward and Lee kicked off his smart black shoes without looking down. He had his back to Kennedy. He did not take his eyes off Pai-Lan as he spoke.

"Murray, you remember you asked me what a Sifu was."

"Yes." Kennedy's voice felt muffled, like a child. It sounded like it was coming out from a tunnel, it was so quiet.

"Well it means Master. Martial Arts, all that stuff. That's what Pai-Lan is." He dropped his body weight by bending his knees. He was moving on the balls of his feet.

"What are you?" Kennedy said.

"We're about to find out." Lee rolled forward as he spoke the words, taking Pai-Lan by surprise. He swept both of Pai-Lan's feet away from under him. Pai-Lan cracked his mouth on the ground, losing a tooth. A stream of blood shot from his mouth. He sprang to his feet and aimed a punch at Lee. Lee stepped to one side, one foot behind the other, blocking the punch with his left hand. He snapped the wrist in one movement. Kennedy heaved. it sounded like someone had stood on a Twiglet in a quiet room. Pai-Lan let out a roar like a wounded dog. He tried to drive his elbow into Lee's face, but Lee was too focused, too fast. Kennedy knew that he'd been waiting for this all the time. He'd probably been thinking about this moment from the day he learned of his brother's death. Pai-Lan should have been more discreet in his bloody business. The elbow missed by a millimetre. It might have been a mile. Mishima stepped forward but Ka-Lut was enjoying herself. She held her hand up to stop him interfering.

Pai-Lan had never experienced this before. Never. He managed to connect with a kick but it lacked the necessary power. It grazed off Lee's thigh as he stepped in and swept the supporting leg away. He stomped on Pai-Lan's shoulder. He screamed. It was a scream cut short as Lee stomped next on his Pai-Lan's neck. It snapped easily and quickly. His head fell to one side like a dead pheasant on a shoot.

Ka-Lut kicked Lee in the face, splitting his nose and sending him spinning across the ground. He flipped back on his feet and aimed a kick at her midriff. It missed by a mile. She was very fast. She spun and kicked him in the gut just missing his ribs which would have split like rotten wood. She hit him with the heel of her hand. It was not going Lee's way. Who knows what would have happened if they had not been joined by some unexpected guests. Ray, Ice, Eyeball, Lex and Big Lip were in no mood for fucking about. They had not been upgraded like Kennedy, and that had not gone down well. No fuss had been made as only Ray with no previous, had been travelling on his own passport. They were armed, heavily. The Brooklyn posse had stayed out of the trouble but had been happy to provide the hardware. That had all been sorted by the other figure standing there, O'Rourke.

"You alright?" he asked Kennedy.

"Yeah."

"I'm going to take your advice and do things softer...after today."

"Maybe you can learn to play the cello."

"Yeah, right."

This was not a time for doing things by half-measure or by the book. Ray put the barrel of the semi-automatic against Ka-Lut's head and pulled the trigger. Not a pretty sight. Dead before she hit the ground. Lee swallowed some blood as he heaved. Lex did the same with Khan and Hung. Felt like they were saving American taxpayers money. No courts, no costs. They let Mishima live. He would be handy to let the others know that the rules had changed.

"Everyone clear off now!" O'Rourke shouted at them. You've only got a few minutes before I call this in.

Kennedy sat down with his hands in front of him, to catch his breath. The stench of death was getting to him. Lee came over and helped him to his feet.

"Where did you learn to fight like that?" Kennedy asked Lee.

His eyes twinkled and he shrugged, "I watch a lot of movies."

"Excuse me."

Lee walked over to where Mishima was standing and slid a sidekick into his midriff. Mishima let out a groan like a wind tunnel.

"So sorry," Lee said.

He walked back to Kennedy. "For my fish."

"Of course," said Kennedy with an understanding look.

Ray and the boys left by one side entrance and Kennedy and Lee left by the other. Kennedy looked over his shoulder at O'Rourke as he left. There was a slight smile on his face. They would never meet again. Mishima was left for the uniforms O'Rourke had called in.

37

Kennedy spent one more night in New York at Lee's apartment. That was longer than Mishima spent in custody. They broke him out. Against all the odds he'd spent a total of four hours behind bars. His rescuers had cut the throat of one guard and the other had barely survived. The dead one had two children. At the airport when he said goodbye to Kennedy, Lee found it difficult to keep his spirits up . The Snakehead were damaged but they would find a new boss. Lee's work was far from over.

The Amati? Well, the violin was never recovered.

Kennedy had a less pleasant flight back across the Atlantic. Virgin did not repeat their generous upgrade. He flew in economy, with the London boys. He thought he had improved but he still hated flying. He felt like he'd been washed and spun with his clothes on.

Once back in Britain, there were no warm goodbyes from Ray and the boys. He was grateful for their help, but he knew that none of it had been done his benefit. It had been for Beverley, Ray's sister. And in the end, Kennedy knew that he had nothing in common with Ray's world.

Beverley had spent time with Cordelia and talked things over with her. She was waiting for Kennedy at the front door of his Islington home. He tried to hold her. He needed to be held. She did not comply. Her coat was on and her bags were packed. She came straight to the point.

"You don't deserve me, Murray. I'm better than what you've given me. You will come to realise what you've missed. You had a good chance with me."

He told the truth when he said, "I realise already,

Beverley."

In a way it was hardly a shock. He'd been expecting it. Milly was at the top of the stairs. She had her chin resting on her hands.

"Come back and see us," Kennedy said.

Beverley looked at Kennedy, then at Milly. "I'll be back to see her."

"Goodbye Sweetie. I'll see you soon."

She stepped out of the front door then turned to Kennedy, "Oh, you'll be pleased to know that your daughter's period of feeling she was nobody was not what it seemed."

"Oh?" Kennedy said.

"Honey, tell Daddy what you told me."

"Yes Beverley," Milly shouted back. "Bye,Bye."

"Goodbye," Beverley said back and blew her a kiss. Then she was gone.

Kennedy walked slowly up the stairs and sat on the step below his daughter. "What are you going to tell me, darling?" He smiled.

She blinked a couple of times and then smiled back.

"I'm nobody, Daddy," she beamed. "And nobody's perfect."

His smile faded as a silent tear rolled down his cheek.

END

For the full range of
X Press titles, check out our
website at **www.xpress.co.uk**

For a full colour catalogue of all the X Press titles, write to:
Mailing list, The X Press,
PO Box 25694, London N17 6FP